Amish Girl Missing

Samantha Collier

Published by Trellis Publishing, 2021.

AMISH GIRL MISSING

First edition. July 11, 2021.

ISBN: 979-8224170128

Written by Samantha Collier.

AMISH GIRL MISSING

SAMANTHA COLLIER

One foot in front of the other, Ada told herself. This tiny little thought kept her going, up the long, long hill. She had walked this hill a thousand times, over the years. When she and Noah had been courting. With Ruth, since she had been a toddler. But this walk...well, it was the hardest one that she had ever endured.

The people fanned out around her; to the side, ahead and behind. All of them, with the same intent. They called her daughter's name, over and over. The fear in Ada's heart was overwhelming. Where was she? How could she have put Ruth to bed, like every other night, then walked in this morning to find it empty?

Her mind cast back to that moment, when the whole world had changed.

She had been preparing breakfast, as she always did. Ruth liked boiled eggs, with toast on the side cut up into pieces, which she would then dip into the yolk. She had put the eggs onto the table, glancing at Noah as she did so.

"Do you want eggs, as well?" she asked.

He didn't look up from the newspaper that he was reading. "*Nein*," he said. "Just coffee will do me this morning."

Ada had opened her mouth, to say something; to try to connect with him. But then she shut it again. What was the use? It had been like this between them for so long now, it was as if she was living with a stranger. Her husband was a stranger, and the only thing that kept them together was their daughter.

She had walked to the bottom of the stairs. "Ruth! Your breakfast is on the table!"

She had gotten distracted, making pancakes. When she had walked back into the dining room, the eggs were still sitting on the table. Ruth wasn't there. With a sigh of irritation, Ada had walked up the stairs, quickly. It was unlike Ruth to sleep in, or be tardy. Usually, her six-year-old daughter was up before she was, hassling her mother for breakfast.

She had walked into Ruth's bedroom. "Time to get up, lazy bones," she had said. And then stopped suddenly, staring at the bed, puzzled.

Ruth wasn't in it.

The quilt was pulled back, and Ada could see that the pillow had been moved in the night. But Ruth was not there. Had she slipped out, to go to the bathroom without her noticing? Yes, that must be it.

She quickly ran back down the stairs, calling as she went. Noah glanced up from his paper, a frown of irritation on his face.

"Ruth!" Ada moved from room to room, her steps quicker as she went. No, she wasn't in the bathroom. It seemed like she wasn't in the house, at all. Had she decided to go to the henhouse? Perhaps. Ruth loved the hens, and would often spend time with them. One of her favourite chores was feeding them, and collecting the eggs.

It was a still, cold morning. Ruth walked quickly to the henhouse. The chickens were all still on their nests, and looked up at her in affront when she walked in.

Ruth wasn't there.

A sick feeling started to overcome Ada. It felt a bit like nausea, but also dizziness. She had to stop, for a moment, and rest her hand against the henhouse to steady herself.

There must be a perfectly reasonable explanation, she had told herself. Don't panic.

Her legs threatened to buckle beneath her as she ran back into the house.

"Ruth is missing," she gasped to her husband. Noah looked up at her, putting his coffee cup down.

"What are you talking about?" he said. He gazed at her as if she had gone mad, and perhaps she had. Even as she said the words, they sounded so ludicrous.

"She isn't in her bedroom," Ada continued, steadying herself against the table. "I've checked the bathroom, the whole house...I even went into the henhouse. She isn't here."

Noah put down his paper, and stood up. "I will check myself." He walked off, calling Ruth's name.

Ada had slowly sunk into a chair, trying to calm her breathing. Noah would find her; she was probably playing a silly game of hiding. But she had never done so before. What was happening?

Eventually, Noah had walked back into the room. He stared at her, his face pale.

"I cannot find her," he said. "Did you check on her last night?"

"Of course I did!" Ada spat out. "Just before I went to bed, I looked in. She was sleeping. I didn't look this morning – I just came down and started breakfast."

Noah looked grim. "She is probably just hiding somewhere," he said. "But we cannot take that chance. I want you to walk around the property again, and I am going to the Yoder's to see if they can help us search."

Ada felt like she was going to be sick. His words – so calm, so measured – brought home the reality of the situation. Her daughter appeared to be missing. She nodded, and Noah put his hat on, quickly walking to the buggy. The horses nickered as he steered the buggy down the track.

While he was gone, she searched around the whole property again, but still no sign of her daughter. By the time that Noah got back, she was sitting on the ground near the vegetable patch, weeping.

He had brought the Yoder's, but also others. She could see them all, milling about, talking to each other underneath their breath. They weren't smiling.

Noah had walked up to her. "Get it together," he hissed, his eyes narrow. "You will do no good sitting on the ground, weeping."

Ada had looked up at him, stung. "What am I supposed to do? How am I supposed to feel?"

He had simply looked at her, then walked back to the others. Ada stared after him, her heart breaking. It was bad enough that this horrible situation was happening, but Noah's words were like salt being poured into the wound.

What can I expect? thought Ada, as she viciously wiped away her tears. He never spoke to her kindly, or with love, any more. Why should I expect it to be different, in this situation? How can I expect that he would suddenly talk to me like he used to?

She had tried to brush it aside, but it was like another kernel of bitterness had entered her heart.

The search party had conferred, and then they had spread out, over the hill. Calling Ruth's name. Searching for her little girl.

One foot in front of the other, she told herself, again. It was simply the only way that she could think of, to get through this nightmare.

***

They had been walking for over two hours, and there was still no sign of her.

An enormous feeling of dread, like a rock, seemed to fall into Ada's stomach. Her legs started slowing down, and then she simply fell, into the soft earth.

She could hear people around her, and could vaguely see their faces above her, but they were darkened, like shadows. Amongst them, she could see Noah's face. Did she imagine concern and love in his eyes? It was all too hard to work out...

The next thing that she knew, she was in her bed. She opened her eyes, to see Martha Yoder sitting beside her, in her rocking chair.

Ada sat up. "Where is she?"

Martha leaned over, taking Ada's hand. "She still hasn't been found," she said, gently. Her eyes were full of compassion. "Ada, you must rest. It has been a big shock for you. You collapsed on the hill, and we had to bring you back."

Ada started to fling the quilt back. "No, Martha! Ruth is missing. I have to be out there, looking for her, along with the others."

Martha put her hand on Ada's arm, restraining her. "It is almost dark," she said, gently. "They have all started coming back. There is no point, looking in the dark. We will try again at first light. There is nothing more that you can do for the moment, Ada."

Ada burst into tears. "I cannot bear it," she said. "The thought of my baby in the dark, alone."

Martha's arms were around her, hugging her tightly. "I know, I know," she crooned. "Hush. She will be found. I have been praying all afternoon for her."

Ada wept into the woman's hair, her sobs so hard and violent, she thought that they would surely tear her apart. It was unbearable. The pain was simply overwhelming, and she could not see a way through it...

She woke again. This time it was dark, and the lantern on her bedside table had been lit. Martha wasn't sitting in the rocking chair. She got up, wearily, putting her dressing gown on. She crept down the stairs on shaking legs.

The house was deserted. All the search party had obviously left; there were still empty coffee cups on the table. She walked through into the living room, where a single lantern was burning.

He was sitting in a chair, staring off into space. Noah. As she approached, she could see deep furrows in his face; he looked as weary as she had ever seen him. He hadn't heard her approach, and jumped slightly when he saw her.

"You should go back to bed," he said to her, staring at her with his dark eyes. They were filled with unshed tears. "Everyone will be back at first light. There is nothing more that can be done, for now."

Ada gazed at him, wanting so desperately to run to him and hurl herself into his arms. If this had happened a year ago, she would probably have done just that. But it had been a long, long time since she and Noah had been affectionate toward each other. Even longer, since they had spoken to each other well. The cracks in their marriage had started appearing slowly, but were now so heavily carved into it, she simply could not see a way around them.

Her heart filled with a fresh burst of sorrow. How had they got like this? How had it all gone so terribly wrong?

She took a deep breath. "Will you be sleeping in our bedroom, tonight?"

He turned his face away from her. "I think not. I will go into the spare room, just the same." He paused. "Ruth's disappearance hasn't changed things, Ada. You know as well as I do that it is all too late."

Ada gasped. Yes, she knew...but why did he have to talk of it, now? When their beloved only child was missing? It was cruel. What had she done to him, to make him act in such a callous way toward her?

He had once looked on her with so much love, it had taken her breath away. The love had been so strong, and there had been so much of it, it was like had been awash with it – she could almost have bathed in it. And now, there wasn't even the merest trickle, to replenish her parched soul.

"As you like," she said, wearily.

She turned away, and walked slowly back up the stairs. She didn't look back.

As she climbed back into bed, she knew that it was inevitable. The dark thought pushed against her, even as her worry for her daughter overwhelmed her.

They were going to divorce.

They had spoken of it, fleetingly. Skirted around the topic, almost as if the mere mention of the word would rip open the fabric of their lives. It wasn't something that was approached lightly, in their community. Very few couples divorced; there had to be extreme extenuating circumstances, to force God fearing Amish folk to break their vows.

The fact that they were even contemplating it, spoke volumes about the state of their marriage. How far the estrangement had progressed, and how desperate they were for some relief from this constant source of pain.

As Ada closed her eyes, her mind drifted back, to the time before. When they had been the whole world, to one another. When they had loved each other so completely, it had seemed that things could never change...

***

Ada had known, right from the start, that Noah Miller was the man for her.

She would watch him, at Evening Sings. His voice was powerful, and he sang with such devotion. To start with, it had been his voice, that had caught her attention, and hooked him into her heart. But she had never believed that he would look on her with fondness; he seemed to not notice her, at all.

But that wasn't the case. Noah was watching her, too, or so he claimed afterwards. Waiting for his moment, to approach her, and ask her to court.

She remembered their first date, as clearly as if it had just occurred. She could feel the snowflakes that had fallen on them, as they had ridden into town, to eat at the restaurant. She could taste the chicken pot pie that she had barely eaten. Most of all, she could hear his voice, talking to her so gently and sweetly.

They had both known, right from that first date. That they would end up together. It was as if it had been written in the stars.

It had been a long engagement, but they had never faltered in their commitment.

And then, their wedding day. It was strange, but she couldn't remember too much about it; perhaps her nervousness had overwhelmed her. The only thing that she could remember, clearly, was walking towards Noah; seeing him there, waiting for her. He was about to become her husband. She was the luckiest woman in the world.

And for a long time, it had stayed that way. They had set up their home, and been blissfully happy. She had expected that it would always be that way. But, she had also expected that a large family would follow, as well. And that hadn't turned out the way that she had thought.

After two years of marriage, there were still no children, and she was starting to get concerned. Noah told her to just relax – Gott would bring them children in his own time. So, Ada had prayed, daily. It had pierced her heart, to see girls that she knew and had grown up alongside, with two or three babies. She had tried to stop dwelling on it, but it seemed to consume her every waking thought.

And, inevitably she supposed now, it had started to affect her marriage. She turned away from Noah, instead of toward him. He noticed her distance, and tried to bridge it. But she was so caught up in her desire for a child, she didn't care. She had thought that the relationship would take care of itself, and that she could spend long spaces of time emotionally away from him, if she had thought of it at all. The truth was, the desire for a child had overtaken her whole life.

And then, a miracle had occurred. She had fallen pregnant, with Ruth. So much anticipation and joy! It had brought her and Noah back together, and she had believed that everything was as it should be.

But, there had been no more children. And she had let the bitterness of that infect her whole life, even her relationship with her only child. She had returned to that state of constant obsession about having more children. The truth of it was, it had clouded her relationship with her only child, and her husband.

Why couldn't he give her more children? Why didn't he understand how she felt? He came from a large family, as did she. It was normal, in their community. It was expected. Having only one child was strange, and she felt the loss of it keenly. Not just for her sake, but also Ruth's. She would not have the brothers and sisters that she needed. It was a lonely life, for a child.

Ruth became her whole world, and Noah was on the fringes of that.

They were in the middle of it, before they even knew. It was as if Ada had woken one day, and there was a stranger, lying beside her. She simply couldn't talk to him, anymore.

He grew more and more distant. He would spend long periods of time away from the house, and when he was there, he rarely spent any time with her. He loved Ruth, and he would spend time with her roaming the hills or tending the vegetable patch. But, it was as if Ada and Noah were two bubbles, drifting along side by side, unable to enter each other's world.

They would sit at the dining table for meals, and not talk. There didn't seem to be anything left to say. And then, one day, he had simply moved into the spare bedroom. They hadn't ever talked about it; she didn't know how to start the conversation. But she felt the loss of him, and would cry herself to sleep at night.

She would pray to Gott, asking how she could mend her marriage. But, there didn't seem to be any answers.

Ruth had never seen any animosity between her parents. They had made very sure of that. When she was there, they were polite to each other. There was no yelling, or fighting. Maybe it would have been better if there had have been – maybe they could have cleared the air. Found a way back to each other. It was as if a layer of ice had settled over them, one so hard it was impossible to crack.

Then that awful word had started to creep in, whenever they spoke to each other, which wasn't often. Divorce. But as soon as it was said, they shied away from it. It couldn't possibly end like this...could it?

All her hopes, and dreams. All her love, for Noah and for their family. About to shatter, completely, like a vase on the edge of a table, where one loud footstep or accidental brush of a hand would see it careering to the floor. Into a million pieces.

He had said it to her, again, just last week, walking past the bedroom. He had stopped, and come in. She had straightened from putting clothes into her drawer, and looked at him warily.

"I think that we need to seriously consider our future," he had said, gravely. "A divorce might have to occur, Ada."

She had wanted to scream, and cry. To shout out that she loved him, and that she wanted to be his wife, always. But she hadn't done any of those things. Instead, she had looked at him, and nodded.

"*Jah*," she said. "It seems that it is the only way." She had paused, and looked down at her trembling hands. Keep them still, she willed herself.

But if he noticed, he ignored it. And then he had simply walked out of the room.

***

Ada must have drifted back to sleep, but she tossed and turned all night. The sun wasn't yet fully risen when she got up, dressing quickly.

Where was Ruth? Where was her baby girl? She sank to her knees, in prayer, beside the bed. Fiercely imploring the Lord to find her child, and keep her safe.

As she walked into the kitchen, she could hear the buggies coming up the track. They had returned. She put on the coffee, and collected as many cups as she could. They would need it, before they started traipsing the hills again.

Noah entered the kitchen, walking over to her. "We are going a different way, today," he said, looking out the window. "To the east. It would be better if you stayed here, Ada."

She swung around to him, stung. "*Nein*! I need to be out there, searching as well."

Noah shook his head. "You cannot do it. It is too much for you. You collapsed yesterday. And what if she were to return home, and there was no one here?"

Ada trembled. Yes, there was truth in that. If her little girl was lost and roaming and somehow found her way home, she needed her mother here. She couldn't return to an empty house.

"If you think it is best," she sighed, gazing at him.

His dark eyes roamed over her face. "I do," he said. "We will find her, Ada. I promise you."

A weight of emotion hung between them, so sad and tender she could almost touch it.

And then, he reached out, and took her hand. They gazed into each other's eyes, not speaking. But it didn't last long. The next thing, people were coming into the house, and he stepped back from her. She felt the loss of his hand so strongly, it was almost like an amputation.

As people crowded the dining room, she sought him out with her eyes. Before they all left, he turned back to her. It seemed as if he was thinking of approaching her, but then he hesitated. The moment was lost.

She watched them walking back up the hill, until they were all tiny pinpricks in the distance.

***

The hands on the grandfather clock moved agonisingly slowly.

Martha stayed with her, and for that she was grateful. Her own family had moved far away, years ago, and could not be here with her, in this awful moment. She could contact them, and tell them, and she knew that they would come, in an instant. But something inside of her resisted it; if she said it out loud to them, it would make it more real.

The two women sat side by side on the sofa, working on their needlepoint. They didn't speak much. Sometimes, Martha would get up, and Ada could hear her in the kitchen. She would bring in coffee, or some food. Ada would thank her, but every time she attempted to eat, it was like it caught in her throat.

In the late afternoon, her work started to blur, and she was unable to even see the needle, let alone thread it through and make stitches. She put it down, standing up.

"I might go and lie down, for a while," she said to Martha. Martha looked up from her own work, and nodded. Her eyes were full of compassion.

She slowly walked up the stairs, towards her bedroom. But then, as if her feet had a mind of their own, she turned, and walked into Ruth's bedroom.

Everything was the same. Ada's eyes took in the lace curtains, that she had made herself. The little wrought iron bed, with the quilt that she and Ruth had made, together. The bed had not been made; the quilt was still flung haphazardly. Ada could see the indent in the pillow, where Ruth's head had lain.

Her wicker chair, in the corner. Her dressing table, where her dolls were lined up, in a row. Ruth would play with them for hours, up here. Her school satchel, with her reader poking out. A faint scent of lavender permeated the air.

A bottomless grief filled Ada's heart, and she collapsed onto the narrow bed, rubbing the quilt against her face. It was too much. It was simply too much. How much sorrow could one heart endure?

Where was she? What had happened?

She heard a soft sound, and flew up from the bed, her heart in her mouth.

"Ruth?" she whispered. "Is that you?"

But it wasn't. The room was empty; the silence overwhelmed the space...

When she next opened her eyes, it was dark. Panic flew through her, and she couldn't remember where she was, for a full minute. Then, the outlines of the room took shape in her eyes. She must have fallen asleep, on Ruth's bed. Her hands were clinging to the quilt.

Her eyes turned to the bedside table, and immediately focused on a cup, sitting there. Puzzled, she sat up, picking it up. It was hot chocolate, and it was warm. Had Martha brought it up for her?

She sipped the drink, feeling the warm liquid flowing through her. But then, her eyelids started to droop, and she sat the drink back down. She should go to her own room, climb into her own bed. She knew that Ruth hadn't been found – someone would have woken her up. But, she found that she couldn't move. She would get up, a bit later...

When she next woke up, she was confused, again. She was no longer in Ruth's bedroom; instead, she was in her own bedroom, tucked up in her own bed. She was wearing her nightgown. How had she got here? It made no sense.

She heard the floorboards creak, in the hallway at the top of the stairs. And then, she saw Noah walking past. He stopped at the bedroom door, staring at her.

Should she speak? But something told her not to. She closed her eyes.

He walked slowly into the room, standing over the bed, gazing down at her. She kept her eyes closed. And then, she felt his hand, on her face. He slowly stroked it, and she could feel love pulsing through his fingers.

One solitary tear fell down her cheek, trickling into her mouth, feeling his hand on her face, gently stroking.

Then, he stopped. She heard him sigh, and then he slowly walked back out of the room.

***

The next day, she dressed, and came down the stairs. The sun hadn't yet risen.

Noah was already up, sitting at the table. He had a coffee, and was sipping it occasionally as he stared out the window. Ada walked over to the table, and sat down. She didn't say anything. She was remembering the feel of his hand on her face last night, slowly stroking her face.

He must have picked her up and carried her back to her own bedroom. He must have tucked her into the bed, and pulled the quilt over her.

"Noah." Her voice sounded croaky, as if it hadn't been used in a long, long time.

He slowly turned to her. His eyes were full of pain.

She gasped, reaching out to take his hand. He looked down at her hand, then slowly he placed his own in hers.

They sat there, not speaking, holding hands across the table, and watched the sun rise together.

***

When the people arrived, to continue the search, Noah and Ada were still holding hands. And they did not release, as people came into the house. They didn't release, as people walked into the kitchen, pouring themselves coffee.

When he finally released her hand, when the search was about to begin again, she felt the loss so keenly she had to take her hand and bury it, in her apron.

"Good luck," she said. It seemed such a simple thing to say; but then, nothing she could say could capture what she was feeling at the moment. It seemed as good as anything.

Noah gazed down at her, his eyes raking over her. Again, she was hit with the force of the love that was within his eyes.

"Thank you," he said. And then they were gone.

She and Martha took up their needlepoint again. The hours stretched on, travelling so slowly it seemed to crawl. At midday, she sat her work down, and turned to Martha.

"I might go for a little walk," she said. "Just to stretch my legs."

Martha looked at her, a slight frown furrowing her brow. "Do you want me to come with you?"

Ada smiled, gently. "I would like to be by myself," she said. She gazed at Martha. "I just wanted to say thank you, Martha. I so appreciate you coming here, and sitting here with me. It has helped me so much."

Martha smiled. "You would do the same for me," she whispered. "Anything that I can do, I will for you at this time. I am praying for you and Noah, Ada."

Ada nodded. She couldn't say anything more; she thought that she would probably start crying, if she did. Instead, she stood up, and walked to the front door, putting on her cloak and bonnet.

She was intending to just walk around the garden. But she found that her feet had a mind of their own. She walked past the vegetable patch, trying hard not to stare at the tomatoes that Ruth had planted with her father. She walked past her beloved rose bushes, that she tended daily when they were in bloom. She walked past the henhouse, noticing vaguely that someone had let the hens out this morning, and they were roaming the yard. She walked past the barn.

She was back on the hill.

No one was in the vicinity; she couldn't even hear voices on the wind. They must have set out in an opposite direction. She kept walking, up and up. She stumbled sometimes, when her feet hit a rock, or fell into a crevasse, but it didn't stop her. She felt possessed with a wild energy, as if she could walk forever.

Until, she suddenly stopped.

"Ruth!" she yelled, over and over. The call was caught by the wind, and reverberated over the hill. But still, she did not stop. She yelled, over and over, until her voice was hoarse. But there wasn't an answering call.

She fell, then. Simply collapsed onto the ground, her chest heaving.

She didn't know how long she stayed that way; the wind grew colder, and shadows of clouds danced on the ground in front of her. She knew that she should get up, and start walking back to the house.

She knew that she had to. But she simply couldn't bring herself to lift her legs.

The sun started to set over the mountains, and the air grew colder. Dusk was spreading over the hill, a messy array of orange and purple, bruising the sky.

All was still. She could feel Gott around her, in every wild flower, in every rock, in every tree swaying in the breeze. His presence was so strong, she felt as if she could turn around, and he would be there, looking at her.

She remembered his son's suffering, and that he had suffered for all of mankind. Somehow, the thought connected so strongly with her she gasped. Suffering was a part of life; there was denying it. Jesus had asked the Lord to take away the cup of suffering. He was fearful in the face of it, the same as everybody was. In this, everyone was the same.

She heard a noise behind her, a slight crack of a twig on the ground. She turned. Noah was standing there, looking at her.

He walked over to her, and sat next to her, on the ground.

"It is a beautiful sunset," he said, staring over the hill.

Ada nodded. "*Jah*, one of the most beautiful that I have ever seen." A slow tear fell down her face as she said the words.

"We still haven't found her," he said, turning his face back to Ada.

Pain pierced Ada's heart like an arrow. She turned to Noah, and saw her own pain, reflected there.

He reached out for her, pulling her to him. They embraced, clinging to each other tightly. They stayed like that for a long, long time.

Eventually, she pulled away a little, resting her head in the crook of his neck. It was so familiar to her, and so beloved. She had missed him, so much.

His hand came to her hair, and started stroking it, gently.

"I'm sorry," he whispered. "I am sorry that we lost our way with each other, Ada. I have never stopped loving you. I don't think that I will ever stop loving you."

"I am sorry, too," she said, her voice cracking. "The distance between us became so wide, I just didn't know how to bridge it. I wanted to, so much! I love you, too, Noah. You are the only man that I have ever loved, and the only man that I want."

She lifted her head, and turned to him. They stared into each other's eyes, love pulsing between them so strongly that she felt it melt into her very pores, and become a part of her. How had she ever believed that their love had gone?

"What will happen?" she said.

"I do not know," he answered. "We have searched far and wide, but there is still no sign of her. But, we will never stop. I give you this vow, Ada. I will never stop searching."

"We will never stop searching," Ada replied. "I want us to do this, together. We must. Ruth deserves no less. She must know that her mother and father are together, looking for her. That together, we are strong, and that she must return to this family."

"*Jah*," he whispered. "Together, we are strong."

They stayed in each other's arms, staring over the hill, until the sun finally set. She could hear the rustle of animals in the bushes, ready to start foraging for the night, and the soft, mournful hoot of an owl. Noah stood up, and gently pulled her to her feet.

"We must return," he said. "It is getting dark, and we must eat. Keep up our strength. We cannot fall down."

Ada nodded. Hand in hand, they walked back down the hill. They didn't speak.

At the house, all was quiet. Everyone had left. Martha had lit the lanterns before departing, and they glimmered through the windows.

Ada walked to the kitchen. A casserole was on the bench, along with a note: "I prepared this for you both this afternoon. God bless. Martha."

Ada smiled, warmth filling her heart. There were good people in the world. She had always known it, but the last few days had shown her, in so many different ways. Martha had been like a sister to her, holding her hand through her darkest hours. That there was such kindness in the world took her breath away.

But it wasn't just Martha. All the people, who had come to search for their daughter. Those who had taken time out of their own lives, to do this for her family. Ada caught her breath, and offered up a prayer of gratitude to all of them.

She stoked the fire in the wood oven, and put the casserole in to heat up. She took down plates and cutlery, and walked into the dining room. She set the table carefully.

When the casserole was ready, they sat at the table, and prayed.

The food was good. With every mouthful, she could feel strength returning to her. Noah ate doggedly, spooning the food into his mouth. From time to time, they would gaze at each other, and smile, gently. The love pulsed between them as strongly as an electric current.

Ada suddenly realised that she hadn't drawn the curtains, and stood up, walking to a window.

"Don't close the curtains," said Noah. Ada looked at him, but he said nothing more.

Her hand stilled on the curtain. Yes, he was right. They needed to remain open. The lanterns needed to be a beacon, in each window. Every night, she would light them, and place them in each window. Every night, without fail. Until their daughter was returned.

Their house would be the lighthouse, calling to her. Leading her to safety. A constant, never changing. A solid thing. A sanctuary, of love and familiarity.

And she and Noah would be standing here, side by side. Hand in hand. Ready for that day, when their daughter's hand would come to join their own, once again.

THE END

AMISH FRAGILE

20

Chapter 1

The fragile man lying in the bed near the window let out shallow breaths as if each one was soon to be his last. Hard lines of a life lived in anger and disappointment mapped his rice papery skin and wispy gray hair exposed his scalp. Beside him, like a statue, was his wife. Her expression revealing a life of heartache and pain and her blue eyes stare vacantly out the window.

"How long do you think he'll cling to this life?" Joseph asked his *mamm*.

Her eyes moved in slow motion, studying him from below wrinkled eyelids, "Until he finds peace."

Joseph could have laughed out loud had it not been for his *mamm*, but if there was one man who had fallen far enough from grace, it would be his *daed*.

Since he was young, his *daed* had been a ruthless man who did things his way. The image he portrayed to the community was in complete contrast to what happened behind closed doors. And although his *mamm* wouldn't even think of saying it out loud, he knew exactly what she thought. She was relieved. Finally she would be rid of the abuse from a man who wouldn't know love if it stared him right in the face.

He had only been six when he had witnessed his *daed* lay into her. She had been out with the women working on the new quilts when he had demanded she return home. It had been the first time he had seen his *mamm* tremble in fear, and it wasn't the last. People did not dare speak of Albert Freud and his bad temper, nor did anyone bother to come to their rescue. Turning a blind eye and pretending to be oblivious was far easier.

By the time Joseph was a teenager, he had followed in his *daed's* footsteps. Equally bad tempered and getting into tussles with other boys, he soon adopted his *daed's* bad habits. It had taken him many meetings with the elders before he tamed his own temper when he eventually turned fifteen. And had it not been for his best friend Abel, who kept him on his toes, he would most likely have ended up like his *daed*, bitter and alone. How his *mamm* stuck it out was only by the grace of Gott.

His *mamm* had gone back to her state of absence, staring aimlessly out the window, and suddenly it was all too much to bear. Fighting the rage that threatened to unravel him, he turned and hurried outside. But even outside, the humidity suffocated him.

"Joseph!" called a familiar voice. "I thought I might find you here," his friend grinned.

"Where else would I rather be," he remarked sarcastically.

Amos slapped him playfully on the shoulder, "You would never guess who I ran into."

He couldn't bother guessing, right now, all he wanted was solitude. "I don't know, who?"

"You remember Grace?"

The name rang a bell but off the top of his head, he couldn't quite recall. "Grace who?"

"Oh come on now, you remember. Grace Smith, she used to live in the *haus* opposite the Bishop."

Joseph's memories came flooding back like a sweet dream. Grace had been a breath of fresh air in a life where nothing made sense. The three of them had been friends since childhood and even as they grew older, they let nothing separate them. That was until her parents decided it was time to move away. He was eighteen then, and she was only sixteen.

"You mean she's visiting?" he asked in disbelief.

"No, she's here to stay."

He couldn't believe his ears, but an uneasy feeling settled in the pit of his stomach. It had been fifteen years since she left, surely she would be married now. And if that were the case, he had no right to even toy with the idea of meeting her.

"When did you see her?"

"Just this morning, she's moved back into their old home."

"Only her, or does she have a family?"

Amos' brows shot up and his buck-teeth hooked over his bottom lip, "You wouldn't believe it. She never married."

This most certainly changed things and Joseph's nerves ricocheted off each other like rubber balls in a silo. So she never married, or maybe she did and it didn't work out, or her husband passed. He found it quite odd that someone like Grace would still be single at the age of thirty-one.

"Is she a widow?"

"What's with all the questions, who cares if she's a widow. What matters is, you have a chance at happiness."

Joseph cupped his hand over the back of his neck, "I highly doubt she would be interested in me."

Amos chuckled and waved his hand through the air, "Give yourself some credit my friend. I bet you she only came back to find you." He rested a hand on his shoulder and then said, "There's a get-together on Friday night at the Bishop's house, and you should come."

Not if he could help it, he thought and gave a nervous laugh. "I'll think about it."

"You do that, I know Grace would be there and I can bet my buggy she would want to see you."

~&~

Grace's nerves were shot; she hadn't seen Joseph for fifteen years, not since the day her *daed* decided it was time to move, all because of Mr. Freud and his accusations that her *daed* had made eyes at Joseph's mother. It had been bad enough that Joseph's *daed* was an alcoholic but the lies were endless. It had nearly torn her family apart and poor Joseph was right in the middle of it all.

"So are you going to the get-together?" Martha asked while Grace unpacked.

"I suppose so."

"Suppose? You don't sound very sure."

She laughed softly, "I just don't know what to expect."

"Grace, everyone knows the truth about you know who? And trust me, no one is pointing fingers at your family."

"Easy for you to say, Mr Freud caused quite a scene back then."

"Yes but we all know what demons he had been facing. He's a deranged man, and besides, he's no longer a threat."

"You mean to say he's passed?"

"Not quite, but he's bed-ridden, it's not too long now."

Grace cupped her hand over her mouth. For Martha to talk so indolently about Mr Freud's condition was shocking to say the least. He was still a human being, and although he was a cruel individual, he was still Joseph's kin. Her heart filled with a sense of sadness at the thought of having lost both her parents in that senseless shooting when they had gone to the city. It had been a criminal and evil act of someone who hated religion, and their aim was directed at the Amish.

"Grace, are you all right dear?" her friend whispered.

She blinked away at the tears and nodded, "Jah, I'm fine, I just feel so sorry for Joseph, Mr Freud is still his *daed*."

"That is true, but there is no love lost there."

"Yes, but forgiveness sets us free. He shouldn't harden his heart so."

"It's easier said than done, did you know Mr Freud used to lay hands on his wife? He was a cruel man and in my opinion should have died..."

"Martha! Don't speak like that, it's not for us to judge," she reprimanded and pulled her *kapp* over her braided long blonde hair before tucking it neatly in. "Only Gott can judge and you don't know what Mr Freud had to endure as a kinner."

Martha sighed dramatically, "I suppose. Now, are you going to the sing or not?"

"Maybe, I will see how I feel."

Her friends moved in for a hug, "You think about it, I'm sure Joseph would be over the moon to see you. We all know he had eyes for you since you were young."

That was fifteen years ago, times had changed, she had changed.

Chapter 2

Joseph stood at the centre of the farm with his hands cupped and yelled. "Sophie!"

After a moment he turned and walked towards the stables and called again. His dog was up to her old tricks again. As he made his way to the row of trees bordering the fence, his gait slowed. He stopped and listened. The wining of pups reached his ears, and he ran towards the brush and there she was.

"Sophie! You silly hund, just look at you!"

He knelt down beside his dog where she lay, with six pups suckling on her. He had tried to keep the stray wandering dog away from his farm but it was in vain.

"What am I to do now?" he said and patted the top of her head, "I can't keep them you know?"

As if his dog understood, she lapped at his hand and Joseph plonked down beside her. He got Sophie a few weeks after his *daed* had taken ill, and she had been his friend since. His *daed* would never have allowed it, had he known. But here where he sat next to Sophie his heart had set off on a faster trot. For a long while he never thought he could feel anything, he had been numb for so long. Nothing mattered until he found her caught in a snare set by hunters out in the forest. When he first found her, he would leave her where she was, but that soft plea for help speared his heart and he couldn't. He wouldn't. He had freed her from the trap and taken her home that day and in the barn he nursed her injuries until she was better. A bond had formed between the two of them there in that musty old barn where he used to hide as a child.

"The old man would drown them all if he could, you're lucky he can't walk."

The pups crawled over each other, wrestling for a teat and Sophie shifted and stretched out and pawed at him.

"We have to get you to the barn," he whispered to his good old faithful friend and looked up at the sky. "It will rain later."

Joseph pushed himself up onto his feet and stretched his legs. "You wait here; I will fetch a crate."

A few minutes later, Joseph was on his way to the hardware store to borrow a crate. But as he passed the bakery, he stopped in his tracks. An unmistakably familiar laughter reached his ears, and he peered through the window. It was Grace, beautiful sweet Grace and other than having filled out into a blossoming woman, she was still exactly as he remembered her. The slight curve of her lips and the dimples that sunk into her cheeks just below the dusty freckles that were scattered across her nose and cheeks was her signature.

As if she had sensed him she turned, her smile never wavering. She looked straight at him and with one hand wiggled her fingers. Surprised he spun around and ducked behind the wall. His heart caught in his throat. There was no way he could face her yet. She had known the good the bad and the ugly of his life, he was broken and she deserved a lot more from life.

Without looking back he rushed down the road towards the hardware store, refusing to look back over his shoulder, but he could feel her eyes burning into the back of his skull.

~&~

"What was that all about?" Mrs Yoder asked as she came to stand next to Grace.

She didn't answer. She too was puzzled by Joseph's behaviour. When they were young, they were inseparable, and now, he could hardly stand the sight of her. Her heart cramped in her chest and she took a steadying breath then plastered on her signature smile.

"I'm sure he was just startled, he didn't quite expect to see me again I suppose."

Mrs Yoder clicked her tongue and shoved the loaf of bread into Grace's basket. "That boy is trouble Grace, it's best to steer clear of him."

"Why would you think he's trouble?"

The older woman shook her head. "As the saying goes, the apple doesn't fall far from the tree."

It was hard to believe, as teens, although she, Amos and Joseph got up to some mischief, Joseph had always been kind and patient. Sure he had his moments where he would get upset over small things, but never to a point that she was frightened.

Puzzled she thanked Mrs Yoder for the bread, paid her and strolled off homeward.

In fifteen years a lot could have changed, and, she too had changed in some way. Life hadn't been easy. Having to come to terms with the cruel death of her parents and finding it in her to forgive the culprits hadn't been easy, but it was her duty as a child of Gott to do so and she did so without question.

Whatever had happened to Joseph after they left? She wondered. Did his *daed* finally get into his head and convince him about the affair? Does he blame her for their misfortune? Sorrowful and downright depressed she hurried home.

Chapter 3

Spring time in Mountain Park was a picturesque sight, pastel colours painted the countryside turning it into a wonderland. But it had been years since Joseph took the time to admire the beauty outside because deep down there was nothing but sadness. Even now that Grace was back in town, he still felt like a lost. There was darkness right there below the surface, which he fought to suppress, an anger festering like an infected wound. *You're cut off the same cloth my boy!* His *daed's* words echoed in his mind. *Adam was formed first; therefore a frau will remain quiet and submissive. It is as Herr Gott instructed.*

It had been drilled into him since he can remember. His *daed* ruled with an iron fist and most certainly did not spare the rod. And thanks to him, he never married or showed any interest in courting. He reasoned if he could avoid any situation that may cause him to unravel like his old man then he would.

Joseph made it to the barn soon after breakfast. A bag of dog food and a bowl in hand with a few food scraps. Sophie was nestled peacefully next to her litter.

"*Morgen* Sophie," he greeted and scratched the dog behind the ear. "How are the *bobbli*?"

She wined and nudged her head against his hand. He felt like a proud parent too, the pups were strong and healthy. He made quick work of fixing the bedding and changing the blanket the pups were on while Sophie ate some food.

"*Ach* Joseph are those pups?"

Grace had come out of nowhere, catching him off guard. He jumped up and dusted the hay from his pants.

"What are you doing here?" he blurted. Realizing his uncalled for reaction, he scratched his head. "Sorry, I wasn't expecting anyone."

"It's all right," she smiled and held out a basket to him. "I went to the *haus* but you were not there, so I thought I'd find you here."

He swallowed. The last thing he wanted anyone to see was what state his *mamm* was in as for his *daed* he didn't really care. "Y-you went to the *haus*?"

"*Jah*," she nodded. "I brought you some cakes. You still like cakes?"

"Cakes," he hesitated, "*Danki*. I um..." He was completely tongue tied.

Grace laughed and looked down at the pups, "May I?"

"No!" he said hastily and Grace stepped away. "I mean, you can look, but you can't touch them yet. They were only born a day ago."

A frown drew her brows together, and he knew straight away he had messed up. "Grace, I'm sorry, I just..."

"It's all right Joseph, maybe I'll come back when they are a few weeks older."

Without uttering another word, she placed the basket with the cakes on a bale of hay and turned to walk away. He should call after her, but he couldn't bring himself to. Already he was showing his character, being rude to her for no good reason. He was better off alone.

~&~

An hour later, Joseph stormed into the house. His frustration was boiling over and he had to do whatever it takes not to go off on some rampage and punch a hole in a wall. He was only angry with himself. Grace meant no harm when she came to the barn earlier. Once upon a time they had been friends, so why couldn't he bear to be near her.

"Joseph?" his mother's soft voice spoke behind him.

"Not now *mamm*," he muttered.

"Yes now," his *mamm* said. "You're not like him you know?"

"*Mamm* I don't want to talk about it."

The frail woman came around the table in the kitchen and peaked in the basket. A soft smile played on her lips. "I see Grace is back in town."

"Yes she is."

"*Das is gut jah*?"

"Nein, it's a mistake. She will make a nuisance of herself," he blurted angrily.

His *mamm* smiled and pulled out a chair, the crumpled up handkerchief clutched in her one hand. "Sit down," she sighed. "I think it is time we talk."

Rolling his eyes he pulled the chair out, scraping it across the wooden floors and plonked down in it crossing his arms and kicking one leg straight under the table.

"I told you, I don't want to talk about it."

"You listen to your mudder, Joseph Freud. I know something is troubling you, and I also know why." His *mamm* reached across the table and touches his arm. "You've spent your life looking after us, and we don't deserve it. It's time you look after yourself."

He tilted his head back and picked a spot on the ceiling to focus on. That much was true, he couldn't leave his *daed* to his own devices. Someone had to stand up for his *mamm*, but even now, with his *daed* on his last leg, he couldn't just walk away. Once his *daed* dies, his *mamm* would need him even more.

"Grace is a sweet girl, and I think it's time you consider taking a *frau*."

"I don't want a *frau mamm*," he spat and then closed his eyes and pinched the bridge of his nose. "I will not put any woman through the same agony you had to endure."

His *mamm* laughed softly, "You think you're like your *daed*, is that it?" she whispered. "Let me tell you something, we all have a choice in life, we choose to be good people or we choose to be bad people. Your *daed* chose his path, and I chose mine. I could have walked away a long time ago, but I stayed."

"And look where that got you?"

His *mamm* stood and walked over to the kitchen window, silence hung in the air before she spoke again.

"Herr Gott has a purpose for everyone and my purpose was to raise and protect you. If I had left, can you imagine what would have become of you?" She asked and turned to face him. "I understand your fear, and I know you are angry. But you can't run away from life because you're scared. Just look at Sophie, how well you care for her and those pups..."

"You know about the pups?" he asked surprised.

"I saw you return with the crate and Sophie in tow, so last night I went to see for myself. Your *daed* would have drowned them, but you, not you. You took them in and made a warm bed for them. You are nothing like your *daed*."

Joseph sat in quiet contemplation for a moment. His *mamm* was right, his *daed* would have drowned the pups or left them out in the cold to die. Maybe she was right, he wasn't like his old man, but that doesn't mean he is marriage material.

"Caring for a *hund* and her *bobbli* doesn't make me a *Maan*."

"No, but it makes you human, and it shows you have *Herr Gott's* character, but most of all, it shows compassion and love." His *mamm* walked towards the doorway and then stopped. "You should make some time for reflection and prayer. Only Gott can show you who you really are."

For a while after his *mamm* had left to go back upstairs, he sat at the table until he could no longer stand the silence. And instead he hurried outside and ran into the field. Surrounded by daisies and other colourful flowers he finally came to a halt. Until today, he hadn't really paid attention to the beauty that surrounded him.

Consider the lilies how they grow: they toil not, they spin not; and yet I say unto you that Solomon in all his glory was not arrayed like one of these. The familiar bible verse crept into his mind as if *Gott* Himself was speaking to his heart. "If then Gott so clothe the grass, which is today in the field, and tomorrow is cast in the oven, how much more will he clothe you?" he recited the rest out loud.

Joseph dropped to his knees, his fingers digging into the soil as sob after sob rippled through him. All this time, he had been trying to do it on his own, and all he needed to do was trust in Herr Gott.

"Forgive me Vader," he prayed, "I have such little faith, I have been trying to be a gut man, but I have failed."

The Lord is near to the broken hearted and saves those who are crushed in spirit.

Here in the middle of the field with not a soul in sight, Joseph, for the first time in years, could hear *Gott* speak and as he spent time in prayer, he could feel his troubles fade away leaving him with one conclusion–He was not Joel Freud, he was Joseph, and he had a choice to be humble and kind.

Chapter 4

It was late Friday afternoon, the street to the Bishop's house was lined with buggies and young men and women along with some older folk strolled casually toward the hall where they normally have their church services. The atmosphere was full of excitement but Grace couldn't help her eyes from wandering about. Although she didn't think Joseph would bother joining the sing, she had hoped to see him there.

"Grace!" she heard her name being called. "Over here!"

She scanned the hall and spotted Martha sitting next to Amos. She smiled and waved, adjusted her *kapp* and then wove through the group of youngsters.

"It's a full house, isn't it?" she said when she reached them.

"It's always like this," Amos grinned.

Grace took a seat next to her friend Martha, her neck stretching to see the entrance.

"Joseph will be here."

"What?" she blinked and looked at Amos.

"You're looking for him *jah*?"

"What, no, I'm just, um, trying to see if there are any other familiar faces around."

Martha giggled. "I hope you ask forgiveness for telling lies. Amos said he saw you at Joseph's place the other morning."

A blush crept up into her cheeks and she looked at them wide eyed. "Are you spying on me then?"

"No, for certain, I was not spying. I went to his house to see the pups, but then you were there," Amos defended. "So why were you there?"

She tilted her chin and looked the other way. "I went to say hullo, is that a crime?"

"Ha, just to say hullo," Martha teased and Grace shoved her elbow into her side.

"Hullo Grace," a familiar voice said.

She swallowed and looked up, and although the bright light behind him obscured his features, she knew it was Joseph.

"Joseph, I didn't expect to see you here tonight."

"I wasn't planning on coming. Hullo Martha. Amos," he greeted the other two. "But I figured it was time I get out a bit."

"Well I'll be... I knew you would come!" his friend exclaimed and scooted over. "You can sit there next to Grace."

Grace could feel the heat from his body radiate and his proximity made her heart flutter in her chest. She was both excited and happy he had decided to come to the sing. Earlier that week when she met him at the barn, she had been convinced that he disliked her and it had left her vulnerable. But now, here where they were seated next to each other, there was a glimmer of hope on the horizon.

It was the strangest thing. When she first returned to Mountain Park, she had no specific intentions, other than to start over, away from the gruesome memories of her parents' deaths. It had only been after she had seen him that day in the street; she realized she still had feelings for him, feelings that were never reciprocated when they were younger. But so many years later, and much older and wiser, she knew her heart and her mind. And both were in agreement. She had strong feelings for Joseph, which was why she never settled down.

"I'm glad you came," she whispered and smiled shyly at him.

Joseph looked at her and returned her smile. "So am I."

The rest of the evening was a great success and a lot of fun. Between singing and socializing, they played games. By 10 PM there were but a few souls scattered in the barn and most people had left.

"This was fun, wasn't it?" she smiled as they too headed out.

He chuckled, "I can't recall when last I had been to one of these sings. Amos always tries to twist my arm to come."

She laughed, "Well then I'm glad he managed this time around."

Joseph slowed his pace as they reached his buggy, "Would you like a ride home?"

Grace smiled, "I'm just up the road."

"Oh yes of course...."

"But you can walk me home," she said at the exact same time and they both laughed.

~&~

Over the next few days, Joseph felt as if a weight had been lifted. Mornings seemed brighter and his nights more peaceful. Every day he looked forward to seeing Grace, and every day counting he grew to like her more.

It was late one afternoon, while attending to Sophie and the pups when Grace arrived at the barn, her expression troubled.

"*Was ist lelz?*" he asked.

"Joseph, it's your *daed*. I went to the *haus* and your *mamm* was crying," she said and took a shaky breath. "She said he's going."

It felt as if someone had poured a bucket of ice water over his head numbing him right down to the core. His old man was finally going and his *mamm* would be free of his abuse forever.

He stood, hands on his hips and looked down at the ground. "Why should I care?" he muttered.

Grace moved closer and placed her hand on his arm. "He's your *daed* Joseph; he needs your forgiveness before it's too late."

"Nein," he said flatly. "He can go to hell..."

"Joseph, do not speak like that. He's been asking for you."

"Why, to tell me how I should handle my wife one day, and remind me how to rule with an iron fist? No, I will not go see him."

The pained look on Grace's face sliced into him like a two edged blade, piercing his heart and he sighed, "Grace, I can't. He had been nothing but cruel to both me and my brother. He even accused my *mamm* of having an affair with your *daed* all those years ago. He ruined too many lives."

Her sad eyes met his, and she reached for his hand, giving it a gentle squeeze.

"I know he wasn't an easy man, you forget that we both used to hide from him when we were young. But Joseph, people change and sometimes it is the realisation of meeting our maker that offers us the chance of redemption." She pulled him by his hand and sat down on the wooden bench against the stall wall and he went to sit next to her. "My parents were murdered."

Joseph turned to her in shock. She said those words so calmly they were almost unreal. "What do you mean they were murdered?"

"I never told you this, but a year ago some fanatic took matters in his own hands, he shot both my parents and they died."

Tears shimmered in those blue soulful eyes and Joseph took both her hands in his. "Why did you not tell me?"

"B-because it would not bring the back."

"Grace, I'm so sorry for your loss." He tucked a stray strand of hair behind her ear. "I don't know what to say."

She looked up at him, her pleading eyes keeping him captivated. "They caught the man who did it. For months I hated him. Joseph, I hated him so much I wanted him to suffer and die, just like my parents did. But as time went by, I realised that only Gott can judge."

Joseph's heart ached for the woman he had come to love. She had so much pain and he was never aware.

She continued, "If I did not forgive them, I would have been stuck where I was. It was the forgiveness that set me free in the end. Forgive your *daed* Joseph. Hatred and anger is like a poison, it kills you slowly, but in the end it kills."

Realisation swept over him and he sat for a moment contemplating everything. Memories flooded his mind, and he recalled every single time his *daed* had taken the rod to him or shoves his *mamm* around for interfering with the way he considered discipline. Out of all the times he could remember he could not recall a single memorable moment. How then can he be expected to forgive his *daed*?

When he eventually made his way home, his *mamm*, and the Bishop was sitting around his *daed's* bed. Grace stood next to him, her hand clasped around his.

"Joseph, your *daed's* been asking for you," his *mamm* said and she came to take his hand.

Not knowing what to expect he moved closer and came to stand next to the bed. Being so close and seeing his *daed* in this fragile state was enough to tear down the walls he had spent years erecting. He looked at Grace and she nodded with a soft smile and saddened eyes.

"*Daed*?" he whispered as he sat down.

There was no response, not even an acknowledgement, and knowing he may never have a chance to tell his *daed* how he feels, he looked at the others. "Can you give me a moment?"

The Bishop, his *mamm* and Grace left the room and for a moment he simply sat, head bowed in contemplation and too scared to take his *daed's* hand. After some time he took a deep breath and reached to wrap his strong hands around his *daed's* limp frail fingers. He felt so cold.

"I don't know if you can hear me, but I wanted you to know, I forgive you," he whispered.

That was all he could bring himself to say as he choked back tears. But it wasn't so much the fact that his *daed* may or may not hear him. To be able to say those three words was all he needed. Suddenly, years of pain and anger disappeared and for the first time in years he looked at his *daed* through different, loving eyes.

There was a soft moan, and he felt his *daed's* fingers twitch under his.

"*Daed*, can you hear me?" he whispered.

His *daed's* lips parted but there was no sound. Minutes later, he drew his last breath.

Joseph sat by his *daed's* side, crying like a small child until he had no more tears left and when he finally got up and walked out to where the others were, he went straight to his *mamm*.

"He's with Herr Gott now."

He drew his *mamm* into his arms and held her close.

Across the room he saw Grace, eyes red and brimmed with tears with her arms wrapped around her waist. She gave him a single nod and a soft trembling smile before leaving the family behind to grieve.

A few months later...

The summer heat was sweltering and cicadas were screeching loudly in the trees. But not even the heat could spoil this day for him. He was about to ask Grace to be his wife, something he never thought he would do. He had resolved himself to being alone for the rest of his days. But Grace had blown into his life like a summer breeze and had changed his entire outlook on life.

Over the past few months, all he could think of was spending the rest of his life with her, and this day was soon drawing near.

Grace had been busy with laundry when he arrived at her house, unannounced. For a while he watched her as she hung the clothes on the line and she took his breath away.

She was wrestling a bedsheet when he approached and took it from her without a word.

"Joseph, you'll scare me to death!"

He chuckled, "I doubt that, nothing can scare you Grace."

She smiled and handed him the pegs. "You'll be surprised. So what brings you here this early?"

He smiled and ringed his hands together before taking off his hat. "Well you see Grace, I... um... well I wanted to ask you..."

"Ask me what?" she asked, and he noted how she held her breath. But a small wine behind him drew her attention. "Joseph is that a pup?" she asked and shoved past him to kneel by the woven basket.

"It's one of Sophie's pups *jah*, I brought her for you."

"She's so small!"

"She's only five weeks old."

Sophie petted the puppy's head and then carefully closed the basket and stood up.

"I'm sorry you were saying?" she continued.

"Well, I wanted to ask if you would consider being my *frau*?"

"*Ach* Joseph!" she exclaimed, "Jah, of course I would!"

Relief washed over him as Grace flung her arms around his neck and hugged him. It was perfect. She was perfect. He hugged her back and whispered. "*Ich liebe dich Grace.*"

"And I you, Joseph."

Ephesians 4:31 – 32

31 Let all bitterness, and wrath, and anger, and clamour, and evil speaking, be put away from you, with all malice: 32 And be ye kind one to another, tender hearted, forgiving one another, even as Gott for Christ's sake hath forgiven you.

A Golden Dawn

41

Terri Downes

A Golden Dawn

Spring came late that year.

Mary could not help but worry a little as she stood outside on the lawn after Sunday hymn singing, shivering in the biting breeze. Surely by now it should have been warmer, she thought. She was concerned about what the late weather meant for the crops, although her father had told her not to worry.

"Worrying is just borrowing trouble," he would always say.

Mary knew that he was right, but knowing did not always help. She worried more than she should. She worried that the weather would never clear, and that the rain would rot the corn. She worried that the winter winds would damage the roof. She worried that her little sisters would catch colds.

She refused to call it worrying. She called it thinking, if anyone asked. "*I'm thinking.*"

Her mother always knew the truth.

"You think too much," she would say. And when she did not speak the words aloud, she would give Mary a look which said them for her.

She was giving Mary that look now.

Mary pretended that she could not see. She stared out at the gray horizon, running her finger absent-mindedly along her forearm, feeling the rise of an old scar beneath the fabric.

She tried not to look behind her, to where she knew Amos would be. She tried to think about the rain, and the corn, and colds, which were things that she could worry about, but not that she could control, so she would not have to do anything about them.

What was about to happen, however, was another matter entirely.

To some extent, this had not been in Mary's control, as it had been mostly arranged without her. She wondered if this was perhaps the reason, that her parents knew that she would think herself into dizziness if they had not simply presented the idea to her fully formed.

She was going courting.

Mary thought about the conversation her parents had had with her, only last week. They had broached the subject a number of times since she had turned sixteen, when the boys in the youth group had begun to take notice of her. It was natural that they should; Mary had blossomed into young womanhood more vividly than any other girl in the area. A number of the boys, with varying levels of confidence, had approached the subject of courtship, and had been turned down one by one.

Each time, Mary's parents had never asked her why she was not interested, only whether or not she was sure. After two years of this had passed, the invitations had lessened, and still there had been no comment. Several months after Mary had been baptized and started sitting with the married women at preaching every Sunday, Mary's mother had finally started to question her oldest child's reticence.

"Are you not just thinking about it too much?" she would ask.

Mary knew that she probably was, but she did not know how to stop herself.

"You could just give one a chance," her mother had suggested.

Mary had given it some thought – too much thought – and had not been able to decide on any one of the young men.

Whenever she started to consider one of them, she would immediately think of a reason why it would not work. One was too aloof, another too forward. Another was lazy. There was always a reason, and Mary could always imagine what might happen a few years down the road. So she continued to say no.

"Do you not want to wed?" her mother had finally asked.

This had been a month ago, while they were working together in the kitchen. Mary's mother had tried to make her question sound offhand, keeping her eyes focused on the pie crust she was rolling out. But she could not hide the worry from her voice.

"Of course I do," Mary had replied.

She tried to explain herself to her mother, who seemed to understand, although by the time Mary had finished she had rolled the pie crust into holes.

"So you do want to," she said again, as though to make doubly sure.

Mary assured her mother that she would love to be in charge of her own household, to have children and run a family.

But with whom? She had no idea.

So it had been something of a relief when her parents had approached her a week ago and told her that they had arranged for her to court Amos.

They had looked quite surprised when she had agreed without a single question. Mary guessed that they must have thought that she would start finding fault in Amos as she had with everyone else. But she knew her parents, and they knew her, and they would have made a good choice, she thought. At least she did not have to worry about it.

She did not know Amos. He had not been one of the boys from youth group to show an interest in her. In fact, she could not remember him ever showing an interest in anything.

Not that Amos was lazy. Mary knew that he worked on his family's farm, and occasionally went to help out at his cousin's farm a few miles away. But the one thing that she did know about Amos – the one thing that everybody knew about Amos – was that he was a dreamer.

Mary had glanced over at him this evening as she had arrived with her family. She had thought that he might be looking out for her, perhaps eager to share a smile at the thought of their planned ride home together afterward. But he was standing to the side with a group of young men, not even paying attention to what the group was saying. He had just been staring into the distance, as though having a completely different conversation in his head.

Mary had thought back to the little she had known of Amos when they were in youth group together. He had always done that, she had thought. She remembered hearing from his sisters that he was often in trouble at home – not through misbehavior, but simply forgetfulness. He seemed not to have grown out of it.

She had remembered, and wondered, and tried hard not to worry.

She was still trying.

The group from hymn singing had mostly cleared; it would be time for them to ride together soon. If Amos remembered, thought Mary. He seemed to be standing off to the side again, on the fringe of another group's conversation.

Her fingers strayed to her sleeve once more.

"Mary."

Mary turned to see her mother looking at her. She reached out and brushed an imaginary speck of dirt from her daughter's shoulder, then pulled the strings on her *kappe* straight.

"Stop thinking so much, child."

"I can't help thinking, *mamme*," said Mary, as she always did.

Mary's mother angled her body a little so she could share Mary's glance towards Amos.

"But if your head is full of what you think of him," said her mother, "how will there be space to learn what he is actually like?"

Mary blinked.

"Look at him," continued her mother. "You don't know him. Don't let your mind fill with thoughts that might not be true. You will find out what is real soon enough."

Mary nodded. She looked. As she did so, Amos turned and caught her eye. He seemed to come back to himself, and smiled.

Everyone else was heading to their buggies when he finally walked over and quietly asked if Mary was ready.

Mary was not sure she could answer that one way or the other, so she just smiled and walked with Amos to his buggy, sparing a single glance back over her shoulder to catch a final warning look from her mother.

As the buggy started off down the road, Mary wondered how other people managed to stop themselves from thinking.

Look at him, Mary's mother had said. The sun was almost gone, but she had a better chance to look at Amos now than she ever had before.

He had the same dark gold hair as the rest of his family, curling at his ears and forehead. His skin was tan, even now, as they made their way out of winter. Light gold. In fact, with his bright, tawny-oak eyes, he seemed gold all over, shining slightly through the gloom of the evening.

He glanced over, and Mary realized she was staring. She quickly turned and looked out of the window, her head filling with concerns that he might think her impolite.

Before the thoughts could take root, however, Amos interrupted them.

"I see the bad weather hasn't deterred the daffodils."

He gestured out to the low bank running alongside the road. It was starred with pale flowers coming up in clumps.

Mary felt her spirits sinking a little. Were they to discuss flowers, now? Was the whole ride to be taken up with polite small talk on subjects Amos guessed she would be interested in?

"I'm glad to see them brightening up the place," she offered.

"I'm not."

Mary paused, confused.

"Why?"

"One of our horses – not this one, the one with the dark mane, you know?"

"Pepper?" Mary dredged the name up out of her memory.

"Yes, Pepper – as of a week ago, he has developed a sudden and passionate urge to eat them."

"To eat... the daffodils?"

"Yes." Amos shook his head. "Just out of nowhere. Every time we take him out, he lunges for them like they're his private horse version of manna. And he gets very offended when we won't let him take a bite."

"Aren't daffodils poisonous?"

"Yes! They are. I have tried to explain this to Pepper, but do you think he listens?"

Amos gave an exaggerated sigh and scowled at the innocent faces of the daffodils they passed.

"I've often found it difficult to get horses to listen to reason," said Mary, keeping a straight face.

"I wanted to borrow him this evening, but I thought he might drag us to the bottom of a field somewhere in search of daffodil snacks. I would have had to pull the buggy back myself."

The visual made Mary laugh aloud. Amos turned a little and grinned at her.

"It's good to see you relaxing a little."

Mary blushed. So he had noticed her tension beforehand. Perhaps this observation should have made her tense once more, but Amos' open expression and friendliness prevented it.

"I don't often do this," she said.

"I know."

Mary immediately worried that he would ask her why, but he did not, allowing a quiet moment to pass.

"I think we all want things that are bad for us," he observed. "At some time or other."

"It's a good test of our character," said Mary. "Although I must say I've never been tempted to eat the local plant life."

Amos laughed.

"No doubt Pepper will have grown immensely in his character by the time the season is over. He'll be the wisest horse for miles."

"I'm sure."

Another moment of silence turned itself over.

"Which do you think is more difficult," asked Mary suddenly, surprising herself, "to want something that's bad for you, or not to want something that would be good for you?"

Amos thought about this for a minute.

"I suppose the second one," he said. "It might be harder to make yourself do something than to stop yourself from doing something. You have to take action instead of staying still."

Mary nodded.

"But it can be just as rewarding," Amos said, and then paused. "I'm glad you agreed to this, Mary."

Mary smiled, enjoying the warmth that comes from being understood.

She smiled again when he asked her if they could ride together the following week, and again when her parents had asked her how it went. She went to bed smiling, for the first time since she could not remember when.

They rode together the next week, and the week after. Amos would come over for his brief visits on Saturday, and for long, lingering talks on Sunday evenings.

The morning after their first ride together, Mary had immediately plunged into worry over the difficulties of getting to know a person from scratch. How long would it take to feel safe enough with someone before you consider spending your life with them?

Sure, their conversation the evening before had gone well, but there would be so much more for each of them to share. How on earth could they get to all of it?

But when she was with Amos, he never gave her a chance to start worrying. He seemed to immediately sense when her head was too full of thoughts, and he would chase them away with a funny story or stray observation.

And when she was troubled and knotted up, he would tell her stories. Long, winding tales that ebbed and flowed and caught every thought in their path. Each sentence would draw Mary away from the threads of worry, serving as a gentle rebuke for letting herself get knotted in the first place.

"What do you think happens next?" he would ask when he got to a bend in the tale, and would not continue until Mary had guessed.

She wondered how he managed to sense her moods. He did not seem to pay enough attention to anything to have developed such keen observational skills.

Now that she was trying to know him better, Mary tried to gauge Amos' interactions with others when she saw him at preaching or hymn singing. His reputation as a dreamer was certainly well earned. He would often lose the thread of a conversation entirely, drifting off and staring at nothing, until someone called his attention.

He then would normally apologize, laugh, and make a self-deprecating comment at which everyone could chuckle.

Perhaps he tried harder when they were together, Mary thought. Or maybe he found it easier to focus on one person at a time. But even though his eyes would drift away sometimes, he himself would remain present.

Mary did wonder, in the first couple of weeks, just how much attention he was paying when she was the one speaking. On the third Sunday evening they spent together, an hour or so into the conversation, she noticed him staring into the fire. She had been recounting a story from earlier in the week. Her little sister Elsa, the second youngest at eight years old, had tried to see if she could fit into an empty barrel in the barn. She had become stuck, and had then been too embarrassed to call for help. The rest of the family had spent over two hours searching for her before Mary had found her wedged into the barrel. It had then taken another fifteen minutes to get her out without risking splinters.

Mary was about halfway through the tale when she was suddenly seized with the conviction that Amos had not been listening at all, and that if she were to stop speaking he would not even notice. So she did.

Amos turned towards her within seconds, his expression confused.

"So where did you find her?" he asked.

Mary paused, irritated with herself for letting her thoughts get the best of her again.

"Wait, you did find her, right? She's not still out there somewhere?" Amos raised an eyebrow in mock concern.

Mary hesitated. "I'm waiting for you to guess what happens next," she said.

She wondered, afterward, what he would have thought if she had told him she was trying to make sure he was paying attention.

Surely people must do this all the time to him, she thought. *He is always staring off at nothing. This must be normal. He should not be offended by someone making sure.*

But something had held her back. Perhaps this was part of getting to know him, Mary thought.

Two weeks after that, he left without his coat. He returned for it twenty minutes later. Mary had seen it as soon as he had left, and was already waiting with it on the porch.

"I thought you might need this," she said, holding it out to him as he walked up the steps.

He stopped one step below her and took the coat, ducking his head a little as he blushed.

"Sorry."

"It's all right," said Mary.

"I think," said Amos, as he shrugged on the coat, " the problem is that I want it to be summer so badly that my mind's started to pretend I don't need a coat. Wishful thinking."

"Just so long as your mind doesn't convince you to try harvesting a green field," warned Mary.

Amos chuckled, his eyes golden in the light of the porch lamp as he looked up at her.

After he had left – for the second time – Mary went back inside. Her father met her as she walked through the door.

"He remembered before he got home, then," he said, shaking his head. "His father was just the same, when we were young. He grew out of it, though."

"Oh?" Mary supposed this was why her father had suggested Amos. He would not have done so if he had thought he would remain so absent-minded.

"*Jah*. And it was never that bad, I suppose. He never... caused any real problems."

Mary nodded. As she walked to the kitchen, she raised her right hand to her left forearm in an old, familiar gesture. She ran her fingertips slowly up the length of her scar, feeling each bump and furrow in the thickened skin.

She was sure that her father had been thinking of this when he spoke to her.

She could not bring it up, though. It would make him so sad.

It had been years ago, when Mary was only six. Her father's grandfather – Mary's great grandfather – had been staying with them since his wife had passed.

Mary had not realized how old he was, thinking him to be a similar age to her grandparents. But although his intelligence and wit were strong, he would forget things. Small things, at first. Where he had left something, what time it was. Then he started getting lost. He would walk off and disappear, and the boys would have to stop work to search for him.

He would always be embarrassed about it. He knew that he was forgetting things, and he hated it, but he could not do anything to stop it.

The accident had happened one morning in early fall. Mary had been working with her mother in the kitchen when her great grandfather had walked in, obviously having one of his far-away moments. He had not responded to her mother's greeting, but had wandered toward the stove. Seeing a pan of potatoes about to boil over, he had reached out to move it, forgetting to use a cloth. When the long metal handle burned his hand, he pulled away with a jerk, knocking the entire pan over and onto Mary, who had been coming over to move the pan herself.

Mary did not remember exactly what happened after that. She thought she could remember someone screaming, though she wasn't sure if it had been herself or her mother. She remembered the confusing brightness of the *Englisch* hospital, and the thickness of the bandages on her arm.

She remembered crying when the bandages had come off – not from pain, but from the shock of seeing her skin like that, like melted wax. The scar ran the length of her forearm, widening from a point on the back of her wrist as it moved up to envelop her elbow.

While he still lived, Mary's great grandfather had always had trouble speaking to her after that day. His gaze would trip over her, trying to land anywhere but her arm, anywhere that would not be a reminder of his fault.

Despite the forgiveness she had given – and given again and again when resentment had crept up on her – Mary had never been able to think of anything to say to him that would make things better.

Her mother had told her, years later, how her great grandfather had asked for help after that, trying to swallow his pride, and how he had so clearly hated every nudge and reminder. She did not want Amos to every feel that way – especially if he did not need to.

So she did not mention it when he was late, and tried not to mind. At least he remembered to come, and was always apologetic when necessary. She did not suggest that he leave a note for himself somewhere, or tie a knot in his handkerchief, even though she wondered daily whether such measures would help at all.

Amos seemed not to mind the lapses himself, always being ready with a joke afterward. And nothing that bad had ever happened. Mary did not want to overstep her boundaries and make him feel as though there was something wrong with him, that he needed looking after.

It would not be worth it to upset him, to have have that golden smile dimmed when she had started looking forward to it so much every week.

Thing continued along in this way for a while. The days began to lengthen and grow warmer. People's talk turned to crops, and estimating harvests. Mary's father and brothers were kept busy planting, the late arrival of spring giving them less time than they would normally have had to complete the task.

Amos spent most of each week with his cousin, who was similarly in need of extra work – his five older brothers meant that he could be spared from his own family's farm. He was full of stories about his cousin's family every Sunday, keeping Mary laughing for hours at a time.

After a while, she began to wonder why he had not yet brought up marriage. They were obviously getting on very well, and things were clearly headed in that direction, but the subject remained untouched.

In an uncharitable moment, Mary wondered if Amos had simply forgotten to ask her.

She tried not to worry about it, but as the weeks started adding up, the concerns became harder to put aside. He would need to ask her soon, so they could prepare to be married after harvest. Surely he did not mean to wait a whole year until next fall?

The answer came along with the summer. Mary often wondered, afterward, if the story would have ended differently if things had not happened the way they did.

It was a low, sultry day, warmth having finally arrived but failed to draw away the clouds. The world looked strange with the sky so dark and heavy, almost as though it were winter all over again.

Mary and Amos had been riding in the buggy for almost an hour. Amos had been telling another story, trying to get Mary's thoughts away from the possibility of a storm. She knew that thinking about the dangers was useless. It was not as though her worries could be used as a covering for the fields to spare them from damage.

So she tried to keep looking at Amos, and not out at the threatening weather. His skin had deepened in shade in the brief span of good weather they had had, and his hair was beginning to lighten. He seemed more golden than ever.

Just what everyone needs on such a dark day, Mary reflected. Their own private sun.

Thinking about this, she finally turned and looked out at the landscape, focusing on the fields and hedgerows instead of the clouds.

The unfamiliar fields and hedgerows.

Her eyebrows pulled together as she tried to make sense of what she could see. The shape of the hills ahead looked a little familiar... but the cluster of trees over to her right was not one she knew, Mary was sure. Yes, there was a stream running over to the left of them, she would recognize that if she had ever seen it before.

"What's the matter?" asked Amos.

"I'm not sure where we are," said Mary. "What turning did you take after the Miller's farm?"

When Amos did not answer right away, Mary felt her heart begin to sink.

"I'm not sure," he said eventually. "I'm afraid I wasn't paying attention."

He reigned in the horse a little, to a slow walk.

"Are you going to turn around?" asked Mary, keeping her tone as unconcerned as she could. "Or keep going until we find our way back?"

"I think... maybe turn around, that seems safest," said Amos, as Mary had hoped he would.

She nodded in relief, and kept quiet as he turned the buggy to go back the way they had come.

She expected him to make a joke or comment, but he did not. In fact, he remained quite quiet for several minutes.

Taking her cue from the way Amos usually managed to soothe her nerves, Mary began talking of her mother's plans for canning in the upcoming months, trying to keep the atmosphere light.

It was not until another half hour had passed that they had to face the inevitable.

"I still don't know where we are," said Mary, hoping against hope that Amos would laugh at her and point out a nearby landmark that was both familiar and obvious.

He did not.

"Neither do I. I think we must have gone down a side lane before coming onto this road. Perhaps one of the lanes leading off that way." He indicated to their left.

"I wish we had bigger hills in this area, or even mountains," Mary commented. "It would be much easier for navigation."

"I bet it would," said Amos absently.

The first lane led to a gate which they had definitely not gone through earlier. Amos turned the buggy again and they headed back once more. It was not until they tried the third turning that they recognized the way.

By that time, what little daylight had been allowed through the clouds was already draining away. Amos put the buggy's lights on without comment.

Mary tried to calculate what time they would get home, and whether they would manage it before her parents started worrying in earnest. Her hands began working at the corner of her apron, folding it into little pleats.

"I'm sorry," Amos said, looking at her expression. His voice was quieter than usual.

"It wasn't your fault," said Mary. "Relax."

"I can't," he said. "I shouldn't."

"What do you mean?"

"I can't relax, this is exactly what happens when I relax."

"...You get lost?"

"I *forget* things. I forget the time, I forget to pay attention. I try so hard to remember everything, but sometimes it's like my mind is water. I mean... well, you know."

"I know," Mary said, unable to deny it.

Amos glanced at her through the gloom which had begun to settle around them, and his expression was pained.

"I know everyone finds it funny, or annoying, but they have no idea how many things I would forget if I wasn't always trying so hard."

"Well, it's only little things," said Mary. "If you're a bit late here and there, what does it matter?"

"No, it's not just little things." Amos took a deep breath, as though to make a confession. "I've lost the horses before – forgot to lock them up, and they wandered away in the night."

"That's not so – "

"Not only once, either. Four different times, I did that. I've missed Sunday preaching before, just from forgetting what day it was. And you know I've been going down to help my cousin at his farm? My mother asked me to take some canning jars along for his wife. The box has been sitting there for three weeks, and every single morning I forget to take it with me."

Mary considered this.

"Couldn't you leave a note for yourself? Or put them by the door, the night before?"

"I shouldn't have to. No-one else has to," said Amos, his tone one of resentment.

"Someone could remind you," said Mary.

I could remind you, she thought. *If we were married.*

"They shouldn't have to," he insisted. "Why should I burden someone else with taking care of me, as though I were a child?"

"Perhaps they wouldn't mind," suggested Mary. *If they loved you.*

"They would," Amos said flatly. "Maybe not at first, but they would grow tired of it. Trust me."

It seemed almost as though Amos was desperate to explain, to have Mary feel the same way he did. As though he needed her to understand – and she did. Finally, she understood. This was why he had not asked her to marry him. He had known of his problems, and he wanted to get control over them before he tried to take charge of a household.

But he did not have control, she could see that plainly.

"You've... well, you've never hurt anyone," she said.

When Amos closed his eyes for a moment, she knew what was coming.

"Last year," he said, "I left the barn door open and forgot about it. The wind blew it shut onto my little brother's hand. He broke two fingers."

Mary remembered seeing little Karl with bandages on his hand last winter. She had assumed it had been done playing.

Her fingers reached up automatically, resting on her scar.

And she was angry. She could not be angry with Amos for forgetting things, for something he could not help. She saw now that she had been right, that he really did mind it that people saw how much he struggled, and that he tried to make the best of things.

She was angry that he had begun this courtship without knowing how it would end, without knowing if he could ever ask her to marry him. Had he thought she would just wait around for him to suddenly change the way his mind worked?

Would he have married her without knowing whether he could handle the responsibility of a family? Would he have done that, knowing that it could be his own children suffering from his forgetfulness in the future? Her children, with fingers broken in barn doors?

And he did not want to burden her with helping him, he seemed to be saying. She would just have to sit by and pray that he did nothing to harm their family.

She held her arm out, turning it a little so her scar was completely visible from end to end beneath the hemline of her elbow-length sleeve. Shadows sank into every crevice, the pale light catching every twist and line in the rough skin.

"Do you know how this happened?" Mary asked.

Amos looked a little thrown at the sudden change of subject, but he shook his head.

"An accident at home, I think you said?"

"I never told you the story, then."

Amos shook his head once more.

Mary told him.

She could not look at him, as she spoke, knowing what this would do to him.

He did not say anything. He did not need to. Mary could see that he understood exactly what she meant by telling him this story. She did not mention him once, never drawing a comparison between his story and hers. But he understood, and he remained silent.

The silence stretched on – not comfortable and spacious, as it had been so many times. It was heavy, stiff, holding each of them in place, sealing their jaws shut.

When they arrived at Mary's home, Amos managed to pull off his usual friendly manner. He apologized to Mary's parents for their lateness, and explained what had happened. He even managed to get her father to laugh when he said they had been ready to send for help using smoke signals.

He said goodbye politely. Mary nodded and wished him a safe journey home. Neither of them mentioned seeing each other again.

As Mary settled herself by the fireside to finish her day's mending, she felt her mother's worried gaze from across the room. She kept her head down, staring at her needle as though it might disappear without proper observation. She knew that if she looked up, her mother would take the opening and start asking questions.

She let her thoughts remain on Amos, on her disappointment and frustration. As odd as it was, she wanted to keep those thoughts present in her mind for as long as possible. She knew that once they faded, she would be left only with sadness.

By the time she went to bed, the process had already begun. Mary lay awake next to little Elsa, lying flat on her back and staring up. Her fingers worked at the edge of the sheet, pleating and folding it the way she did to her apron when she was nervous. Her anger betrayed her by melting away, and she was left thinking about how quiet Amos had been as she had told him the story.

Too many thoughts. They whirred around her like moths, fluttering against the edges of her mind, keeping her awake.

She wished that this had happened sooner, before she had grown to know Amos so well. Then she wouldn't have known how badly he'd been hurt.

No, she wished that she had never agreed to this courting in the first place.

She closed her eyes for a moment, imagining that.

Then she opened them and took the wish back.

No, she would not wish away the time she had spent with Amos. Even with all this trouble, she could not wish away the stories and the silences and the laughter.

And what does that mean? Mary wondered. Did it mean that marrying Amos would make any trouble worth it?

And it would be trouble, Mary thought. It would be a lot of work, making sure that Amos did not drift away from his duties, that everything was kept safe and running smoothly. Not so much work as he had seemed to think – not so much as taking care of a child, she knew that from caring for her two sisters and three brothers as they had grown up. But she would need to always think ahead, checking in with Amos constantly. And once they did have children, it would be even more work. There would be risk.

As Mary lay still, staring up into the darkness above, she finally asked herself: would that make it impossible? Or just... hard? Could she commit to this in the same way she would commit to having children, or to making breakfast every morning?

She knew, now, what she would be agreeing to. It would be an informed decision. But, Mary reasoned, if Amos were to become hurt in some way after they had been married – God forbid – she would be willing to care for him. Even if he were bedridden. And this would not be nearly so difficult.

The problem, really, she thought, smoothing the crimped edge of her sheet back down, was whether or not Amos would be willing to let her help.

Was he really just worried that she would not be able to love and respect him if she had to help him in this way? Or was he too proud to accept the help in the first place?

That was not something that Mary could answer.

She sat up. No, she could not answer that – only Amos could.

Mary slid quietly out of bed, careful not to wake Elsa. She felt carefully for her clothes, picking them up and carrying them with her downstairs. Glancing at the clock in the hall, she saw that it was only half an hour past three – she had thought it was later.

No matter, she decided, as she dressed in the kitchen. She would make the time pass.

It was the earliest she had ever started on her morning chores, but it felt good to work and clear her head. She laid the wood and kindling in the stove, ready to be lit, then set the breakfast things out, ready to be used when everyone came downstairs. She swept the kitchen floor – and then took a candle and swept the hall, being as quiet as she could. She knew she was probably doing a bad job in the wavering half light, but this was more for her own sake than necessity's.

She had just finished a completely unnecessary scrubbing of the counter tops when her mother came into the kitchen, a bemused expression on her face.

"Did the sun forget to rise this morning?" her mother asked, a smile tugging at the corner of her mouth, "or have you forgotten how to tell the time?"

"I couldn't sleep, *mamme*."

"Hmm."

Mary's mother walked past her and busied herself lighting the stove.

"What time is it?" asked Mary, realizing that she had not checked the clock since sweeping the hall, suddenly worried that she had left it too late.

"Five o'clock. Why?"

"I... have to run an errand," said Mary, grabbing her shawl. "Is that all right?"

"Is this anything to do with why you looked so miserable last night?" asked her mother.

Mary nodded hesitantly. Her mother smiled at her.

"Don't be too long," she said.

When Mary slipped out of the kitchen door, the sky was just beginning to lighten. Yesterday's clouds had blown away in the night, and the sky stretched high and colorless above her.

Amos had told her he normally left home at half past five every morning in order to get to his cousin's farm by the time the work started. And his home was a little over a mile away... yes, there was time.

She heard Amos' voice in her head, asking: *what happens next?*

As she walked, rather than batting away worries that flew around her head, Mary made plans. How to help someone remember to close a door, she wondered. Perhaps a mark in the door frame, at eye level, as a reminder. Or perhaps the person could do something every time they closed the door. Like tap it twice, or say a word to themselves, to help solidify the memory of closing it.

And remembering what work needed to be done – well, why not a list? It could be written out every morning, and have every item crossed off when the job was completed, just like Mary had used to do with her school tasks.

We could try a few different things, Mary decided. *And see what works.*

...If he is willing.

Even sooner than she had thought, Mary found herself at Amos' family home. She hoped that she had timed this correctly. She did not want to have to knock on the door, that would definitely embarrass Amos.

It should be about the right time, she thought, noting light at the kitchen window. If he is not late...

Mary heard a door open and close, and recognized Amos through the dim light as he walked down the path. She stepped out toward him. He stopped dead, and Mary took a moment to enjoy his slightly stunned expression.

He opened his mouth, but Mary spoke first.

"The jars."

"Uh... sorry?"

"You need to take the jars, for your cousin's wife."

Amos glanced down at his hands as though expecting to see a box of jars suddenly appear. Then he looked back up at Mary and gave his head a short, sharp shake, like he was not sure whether he had really woken up yet.

He spoke slowly. "You're here to..."

"To remind you to take the jars. The poor woman's been waiting for three weeks, Amos," said Mary.

She spoke breezily, but studied his face as she did so, watching carefully for signs that he would be angry. If he was, she knew that she would have to just let things be. Go home and tell her parents that it was not going to happen.

What happens next?

He did not look angry. A little sheepish, perhaps.

"Thank you," he said.

Mary tipped her head to the side.

"No, really, thank you." Amos nodded earnestly. "For going to the trouble."

"No trouble," said Mary.

Amos raised an eyebrow.

"Well, yes, it was," admitted Mary. "But it was a trouble I was willing to take. That I wanted to take. I want to help."

"Really," said Amos.

He still did not look offended, Mary thought, relieved. Though he did look doubtful. She tried to explain.

"Yes... I've been coming up with ideas. I think they'll work – I think that I can help you. If you let me."

Amos looked at her for a long moment, until Mary began to wonder whether was

going to say anything at all. Then he swallowed, glancing up to the sky for a moment before speaking.

"...And you really think you could do this, and not grow tired of it?"

Mary took a deep breath.

"Some work is more rewarding than others," she said.

Amos smiled at her, his broadest smile, the edges of his eyes creasing. Mary found herself smiling back. She felt as though she were watching a sunrise, light diminishing the shadow inch by inch.

"Although you could make it easier," she could not help adding.

Amos blinked a little.

"What do you mean?"

"I mean if we were married, I wouldn't have had half an hour's walk to remind you about the jars."

Amos laughed, then. And everything was golden.

Samuel and Sarah

Eliza Baker

Part One:

Sarah King flicked the reins of the buggy, urging the horse to move faster. She huffed out an impatient breath. Didn't the creature understand how important it was for her to get to the Troyer house? Today was the hardest day of the year, she had no doubt about it, and she needed to be there for them. It was just too bad that Samuel wouldn't be there as well.

Sarah shook her head to clear out all thoughts of Samuel. Today she would focus only on Mrs. Troyer and the memory of Amos. Just thinking about the younger boy brought a smile to her face. He had been such a good kid, but even he had managed to get caught up in the wrong crowd when he went into his rumspringa years. Headstrong and impulsive, those had been the qualities that had ultimately been his downfall. But he'd also been sweet and funny, and he'd been as close to Sarah as her own little brothers.

A car horn startled Sarah from her thoughts, just a moment before the vehicle swerved around her, causing the horse to shy away from the side of the road. Sarah was thrown to one side of the buggy, and slammed her shoulder into the door, which swung open at the pressure of her body. It all happened in a split second, and for a moment Sarah was thrown into such a panic that when she looked out the windshield of the buggy she thought for certain that she had seen Samuel behind the wheel of the car as it hesitated along the side of the road for a moment before speeding away.

Once the car gunned its' engine, though, Sarah was brought back to the present moment, and jumped into action. She righted herself, took firm grip of the reins, and pulled the door firmly shut. Once she'd slowed the horse to a walk, she took a few calming breaths, and set her mind straight. Surely she couldn't have seen Samuel. He never would have been driving a car, and on the off chance that he would, he wouldn't have been reckless. That was not an adjective that anyone ever would have used for Samuel, not once. No, something like reckless would have been used for Amos.

"And Samuel never would have left me," Sarah whispered to herself, taking another calming breath.

Still, the nagging feeling that she had just seen Samuel for the first time in a year lingered as she drove the rest of the way to the Troyer house. When she pulled up the driveway, Simon, whom she hadn't seen in months, ran from the house to take the horse to the barn.

"You look well, Simon," Sarah said as the thirteen year old helped her done from the buggy. How like Amos he looked, she realized with a sudden gasp of recognition. And how like Samuel.

"*Danke*," he said with a grin that was still just as lopsided as it had been when he was a little boy. Seeing that made Sarah feel like she could relax a bit. He still had some time to be a child before he would go out into the world to experience his rumspringa years. Before Amos died, Sarah had never thought of the running around years as anything dangerous. Her own had been sedate. Sure she had attended a few parties, but for the most part she had just gone to extra sings and socials. Now, though, she saw danger at every turn.

She paused to watch Simon walk off toward the barn before she headed into the house. Looking up toward the front door, she realized that it had been far too long since she had visited. Right after the robbery, right after Amos had died, Sarah had been around the Troyer farm all the time. Later she realized that it had been her way to make up for Samuel's absence, but eventually she had to get back to her own life, helping her own maemm and daed with things around the farm.

Sarah didn't even have a chance to open the door before Lucy, the youngest of the Troyer brood, yanked the front door open, and with a squeal launched herself at Sarah, wrapping her in a vise-like hug.

Startled for the second time in the past half an hour, Sarah felt herself reacting like she was stuck underwater, and she gently wrapped her arms around the little girl. Lucy also seemed to have aged in the time since Sarah's last visit to the family. Had it really been that long? Surely she was just shaken up still from her run in with the car. Her brain was addled, that was all. But when she held the little girl at an arm's length, the child really did look older. She supposed that losing a sibling would make anyone age faster, and she silently said a prayer of thanks that her own family had been blessed with one another. The moment she said the prayer, though, she felt guilty for taking her own good fortune as anything that she deserved. The Troyer family certainly hadn't deserved to lose Amos.

"Sarah, are you okay?"

Sarah blinked and looked down into the concerned face of the little girl. Then she blurted out the first thing that came into her mind. "I think I saw Samuel driving a car! He almost hit me!"

Part Two:

"Tell me again what exactly you saw," Mrs. Troyer said, leaning forward on the sofa, and clasping Sarah's hand.

Sarah's stomach clenched as she realized that the way Mrs. Troyer was looking at her was how she had felt underneath the shock and anger: desperate hunger for news of Samuel. Even if what he had done was awful.

With a deep breath, Sarah repeated the story, adding at the end, "His hair was shorter, but he just looked like Samuel."

Mrs. Troyer clutched Sarah's hand tighter, and Sarah felt her heart stutter as doubt flooded her. Why had she opened her big mouth? Surely this wouldn't make things better for the Troyer's, and she knew that she would have to repeat the whole story for Mr. Troyer.

"It probably wasn't him," Sarah said lamely, gently pulling her hand away from Mrs. Troyer's so that she could clasp them together. She was suddenly shaking. She had been so angry, but also excited in a way at the thought of seeing Samuel after a whole year that she hadn't thought about the repercussions her words would have. "I-I don't even know if he drives."

"He does."

Both women turned toward the sound of a voice in the doorway. Simon stood there, his hands in his pockets and his head down. The way his blond hair fell over his forehead made him look exactly like Samuel had when they were young, and Sarah felt so many emotions that she couldn't even name them all.

"What?" Sarah asked.

"Samuel drives. I think he has a red car now. He's had two over the past year," Simon said, looking up.

"How do you know that?" Mrs. Troyer demanded. Her voice quavered as she spoke, and at first Sarah thought that it was because she was still upset, but then she realized that the older woman was angry at her son for withholding information from her.

Simon shrugged. "I see him once a week. He takes me for ice cream when I take the money from the roadside stand to the bank."

"And how long has this been going on?" Mrs. Troyer asked, her eyes flashing as she held onto her barely controlled anger.

"Six months? I ran into him downtown," Simon said, taking a step back. Sarah could tell that the younger boy knew he was in trouble, but she could also see the stubborn set of his jaw that again reminded her of Samuel.

Mrs. Troyer was silent for a long time, and then she asked, "Why haven't you told us about this?"

Suddenly tears began to roll down Simon's cheeks. "Because I thought you and Daed might make me stop seeing him. I was just so excited to see him, and once he started taking me out every week, I just didn't want it to stop."

"Oh, Simon," Mrs. Troyer said, holding out her arms. The boy flew into her embrace, and sobbed for a minute before he started to calm down. "Your daed and I wouldn't want to take your brother away from you." She froze as soon as the words came out of her mouth, and Sarah felt her heart break for the woman. It had been a bad word choice, and from the way Simon stilled, she knew that he had realized it too.

In the silence, Amos seemed to fill the room. He had been gone nearly a whole year, and yet for a moment he shimmered back into existence. Simon took a deep breath, and stood up, swiping at his cheeks. "I'm sorry that I lied to you, Maemm," he said. "Samuel misses all of us terribly, but he just can't bring himself to come home."

"What is he doing now?" Sarah asked quietly.

"Maemm!" A shriek from the other room drew Mrs. Troyer's attention away from the conversation. Though she looked hesitant to leave, she hurried toward the sound of Lucy's distressed voice.

"What is Samuel doing now?" Sarah repeated, looking directly at Simon.

"He's painting houses," the boy offered.

"Does he have a girlfriend?" As soon as the words left her mouth, she flushed. Why had she asked? Wouldn't it be better just not to know? And yet, she needed to know. She and Samuel were as good as engaged before the...incident, and everything had changed.

Simon shook his head. "No, not that he's said." The boy paused. "Are you still waiting for him?"

The question took Sarah by surprise. Was she? She supposed that her life had been on hold for the last year, and that she had been guarding her heart. She just hadn't thought about it that way before. Whenever she had thought about Samuel, she had shut down her line of thinking so that she would be safe.

"I don't know," she admitted, pressing her clasped hands between her knees. "I suppose in some ways I am."

There was a silence, and Sarah realized that Simon was embarrassed to have asked the question. Sarah wanted to ask him why he had asked, but she didn't want to see him turn as red as a tomato.

"He asks about you a lot," Simon said after the silence had stretched farther than was comfortable.

Sarah's head snapped up. A flicker of hope zipped across her chest. She wasn't sure why she was putting herself through such torture.

"Does he?" she asked as lightly as she could, but she was sure that the boy could hear her heart practically beating out of her chest.

"Every week when we go for ice cream," Simon said, nodding happily. In that moment he looked like such a little boy that her heart ached for him. The whole family had lost so much in the past year, she had lost so much in the past year, and it seemed to her now that none of them had actually been able to grieve and move on, least of all Samuel.

Before Sarah could say anything else, Simon jumped up, and raced to the window. A smile lit the boy's face, and he turned back toward Sarah with a light in his eyes that she hadn't seen in a long time. "He's here!" Simon exclaimed as Sarah heard a car engine outside. "Samuel's here!"

Part Three:

Mrs. Troyer came running at the sound of Simon's cry with Lucy following closely at her heels. "He's here?" she asked, the disbelief in her voice heartbreaking.

Sarah sat frozen to the sofa cushion, rocking herself gently back and forth. Facing Samuel. That was something she hadn't thought that she would have to do. Ever. That hadn't seemed like a possibility. Now that his arrival was imminent, she didn't know what to do.

"Samuel!" Mrs. Troyer cried as she ran out the door.

The conversation grew muffled as the front door swung shut behind the family as they piled out onto the porch. Sarah finally found her courage, and she stood, going to the window. Sure enough, there was the red car that had nearly run her off the road. And there, leaning against it, his arms crossed over his broad chest, wearing jeans and a t-shirt was Samuel. His hair was cut much too short, and he looked entirely too much like an Englischer, but Sarah didn't care. Samuel was mere feet away, and everything in her wanted to run to him. She kept herself still, though.

For a moment, Samuel's gaze flickered up to her, and Sarah felt her heart freeze, despite the heat that she could see in his eyes. Chills raced up and down her spine, and without realizing it, her hand flew up to fix her kapp. Despite everything, she still very clearly cared what he thought of her.

When he looked away, she could feel the absence of his gaze, and she wrapped her arms around herself. Samuel said something to Lucy, and a moment later, the little girl burst in to the house. "Samuel says he needs you to come outside," she called to Sarah.

Irritation flared in Sarah, but she followed Lucy out to the porch. Being so near to Samuel made Sarah jumpy, but she forced herself to keep her step steady. Mrs. Troyer had one hand clinging to the porch railing, and had her other arm wrapped around Simon. Tears stained her cheeks, and Samuel wouldn't look directly at her.

"Sarah," Samuel said when she was close enough. "You're okay."

She took a step forward. "You knew that you nearly hit me? And you didn't even stop?"

"You didn't stop?" Lucy echoed.

"I came here to check on you," Samuel said, lamely.

"What if I had been hurt?" Sarah demanded. "You wouldn't have even know that I was hurt."

"I—I looked in the rearview mirror," Samuel said, running his hand through his short hair. "Wait, that didn't come out right."

Sarah's anger flared brighter. "Gee, thanks," she said. "It's good to know that I'm at least that much to you."

Mrs. Troyer seemed to sense that the two of them needed privacy, so she gently tugged the younger two children into the house. When the front door clicked shut, Sarah turned her angry eyes toward Samuel.

"How dare you," Sarah said, smacking both palms against the railing. "I could have been hurt, or worse, killed! And you didn't even stop to check on me. You knew it was me, and you didn't even stop.

Not that I would condone you not stopping for anyone, but I thought that I meant more to you than that."

Samuel turned away. "I'm good at hurting the people I love," he said.

His words hit her squarely in the chest, and she was stunned into silence for a moment. What could she say to him that would ease his pain? "You can't still be blaming yourself for what happened with Amos?"

From the way he whirled around to look at her, she knew that once again she should have kept her mouth shut. Normally she didn't think of herself as a tactless person, but today she had been sticking her foot in her mouth over and over again.

"I will always blame myself for Amos' death because it was my fault. No one else could have stopped what happened, but I could," Samuel said, his voice breaking as he looked down at the ground.

Sarah took a step toward the stairs, but she stopped herself. What would she do when she got to the bottom? Wrap her arms around him in a hug like she longed to do? She doubted that would happen so she forced herself to stay put.

"How could you have stopped it?" she found herself asking. If she was going to keep throwing her tact to the wind, then she might as well go all out.

Samuel didn't say anything. He just looked down at the ground again. "I should have stopped to check on you," he said softly. "I didn't because I was afraid that the same thing that had happened with Amos would have happened with you. And if anything had happened to you I never would have been able to forgive myself, maybe more that with Amos."

"I—I don't know what to say, Samuel," Sarah said finally. "It's been so long."

"It seems like yesterday," he said, finally looking up.

Sarah didn't know what to do. Anger still simmered just beneath the surface, but she also felt her heart breaking at the thought of Samuel hurting. There had to be some way to ease his pain, even though she was still furious with him. The two of them continued to gaze at each other in a way that made Sarah realize that even after a year apart, their connection was as strong as ever. She opened her mouth to tell him as much, but she never got the chance.

"Someone, Samuel! Come quick!" Simon yelled as he raced across the driveway from the barn. "Daed collapsed in the barn! He needs help! Please come now!"

Part Four:

Sarah raced on Samuel's heels to the barn where they skidded to a stop beside the slumped over body of Mr. Troyer. Samuel dropped to his knees, and with a look of anguish on his face, said, "Daed, please, wake up."

Sarah's natural practicality kicked in, and she dropped down to the barn floor as well, hay sticking to the front of her dress. She felt along Mr. Troyer's neck. When she felt his pulse, she breathed a sigh of relief. "He's got a pulse," she announced. "Is he breathing?"

From the way Samuel stared at her, she wasn't sure that he had actually heard her. He looked so forlorn that she wanted to comfort him, but she knew that she needed to focus on the matter at hand. *Dear Lord, please guide my hands so that I can help Mr. Troyer. Guide my words so that I don't make things worse for anyone in this family. Open my heart so that all anger can leave, and I can let love back in. Amen.*

"He's breathing," Simon reported, leaning close to his daed's chest. Sarah wasn't sure when the younger boy had arrived, but he seemed to have a knack for turning up when he was needed.

"Okay, good," Sarah said. She looked back at Samuel. "We need to get him to your car. Do you think you can lift him?"

"Huh? Oh yes," Samuel said. He seemed to be in a daze, and she hoped that he would be able to drive because that was definitely not something she would be able to do. And running to the nearest phone to call for help would take longer than driving him to the hospital themselves.

"Simon, you help support his other side," Sarah instructed. She was going on her gut instinct as to what she should do. She knew that the Lord was guiding her because she was scared out of her wits. There was no way she wanted to let any more tragedy befall this family. They meant too much to her.

Somehow Samuel and Simon managed to get their father to the car, and slumped him into the back seat. Sarah saw Mrs. Troyer standing on the porch, her hand pressed against her mouth. She was holding back her tears again, but Sarah could see the fear in her eyes.

"I'll be right back," Sarah told Simon. She raced back up the steps, and grasped Mrs. Troyer by the arm. "He'll be okay. Simon and I are going to go with Samuel," she said. "I'll call the neighbors with an update, and if you need to come down to the hospital someone will get you right away."

"Thank you, dear," Mrs. Troyer said as Lucy came and wrapped her arms around her maemm.

Simon had squeezed into the back with his daed, and Sarah slid into the passenger seat. Samuel was fumbling with the keys as he tried to get them into the ignition. She wished that she could take over for him, and if this was a horse and buggy, she would, but she couldn't so all she could do was reach across the center console to squeeze his hand.

As they pulled out of the driveway, Samuel reached over and squeezed her hand back. The two of them sat with their hands intertwined as they raced through the country lanes toward the hospital in town.

When they arrived at the emergency department, Sarah tumbled out of the passenger seat, and ran into the reception area. She looked at the nurse who was sitting behind the big desk, and said, "Please help me, my friend's daed, his father, I mean, passed out. We don't know what's wrong with him, but he needs help."

The nurse set things into motion, and soon two paramedics were wheeling a stretcher out to the car to get Mr. Troyer. Sarah slid down into one of the hard plastic waiting room chairs as the smell of antiseptic hit her nose. Simon slunk into the waiting room, and slipped into the chair beside her. He nestled his head in her shoulder, and she put her arm around him. The Troyer boys, and eventually Lucy, had been closer to her in many ways than her own siblings.

"Is Daed gonna be okay?" Simon asked, sniffling as he tried to keep his tears at bay.

"They are going to do everything they can to make him better," Sarah said.

Simon was quiet for a long moment. Then he said, "They couldn't save Amos, though, could they?"

A lump formed in Sarah's throat, and she tried to swallow past it, but when she spoke her voice came out as a squeak. "Sweetie, they didn't ever get the chance to try. The...bad men who did that to your brother didn't give anyone a chance to save him."

"But you and Samuel are giving the paramedics a chance to save Daed now, aren't you?" Simon asked.

Sarah shifted on the plastic seat, and the crinkly sound made Simon smile a little. "We're doing our best."

As she hugged the boy closer, she thought back to that awful night when they had sat up in the emergency department waiting for news of Amos. Samuel had paced the waiting room until he had left, run away. And that was the last time she had seen him for a year. Sarah's heart seized in her chest, wondering if that was why he hadn't come in yet. Was he remembering that awful night too? What was she thinking? Of course he was. She needed him not to run away again. His family needed him more than he could ever have known.

The doors to the waiting room slid open, and when Samuel walked in, he looked wild-eyed. Sarah breathed a sigh of relief. "Samuel, come sit beside me," she said, reaching out her hand. When he took it, and sat back down beside her, she breathed out another sigh of relief. Somehow now she knew that now they could all finally start healing.

Part Five:

After the doctor had allowed them back to see Mr. Troyer, who was apparently suffering from pneumonia. Thankfully he would be okay, but there was no doubt that if he hadn't been found that something worse might have happened. Samuel had come back just long enough to see with his own eyes that his daed was okay, and then he retreated to the waiting room.

Simon tugged the flimsy curtain back around his daed's bed after his older brother left, and Sarah had wrapped her arms around the boy again. The two of them had stayed until the doctor had shooed them out with the promise they could come back once Mr. Troyer was settled in a room.

"Is he still okay?" Samuel asked when they emerged again into the waiting room.

Before Sarah had a chance to answer, the waiting room doors slid open, and Mrs. Troyer rushed in with one of their neighbors. Sarah peered out the large glass doors and saw a taxi pulling away. She wished that she had sent Samuel back to get his maemm. A taxi was surely more expensive than the family could afford, but she couldn't focus on that now. The most important thing was that Mr. Troyer would be all right, and the family was there together.

"He's okay, Maemm," Simon said. "He has pneumonia, and he has to stay overnight so he can get antibiotics. We can go up to see him after he has been settled into a room."

Sarah felt a swell of pride to see how old Simon was acting, how he had grown up seemingly in a minute. Mrs. Troyer must have seen it too because she crossed the waiting room quickly, and wrapped her arms around her son.

When Sarah turned to look up at Samuel, she was surprised to see the hard line of his mouth twisted into not quite a frown, but close enough. "I have to go," he said.

Her heart sank. He was running away again. The look of sadness and disappointment on Mrs. Troyer's face mirrored what Sarah felt in her own heart. Something stirred there, and she felt the prompting of the Lord.

"I'll go with him," she said in a low tone to Mrs. Troyer who gave her a grateful look.

"Samuel!" Sarah called as she chased him out of the waiting room.

The day had faded into dusk, and the soft purple twilight was still warm. Sarah felt the pins from her kapp pull free, and she had to hold it on with one hand so that it wouldn't fly away. With her free hand she kept waving at him.

"Samuel!" she called again.

"What?" He wheeled around on her, and she had to swallow to keep her courage. Her Samuel was still there under the gruff Englischer exterior.

"I'm coming with you," she said, ignoring the look that he was giving her, and walking to the passenger door of the car. While she waited for him to unlock the car, she watched him out of the corner of her eye. He had set his jaw, just like she had known he would, just like he had done the whole time they had been growing up. It was one of the many small things that she had always loved about him, and she always would.

"Fine," he said finally. As they got in the car, he added, "I can't promise that you'll like where we're going, though."

Sarah shrugged as she got in car and buckled her seatbelt. "I just want to spend some time with you," she said, deciding to continue her streak of bluntness. "Besides you owe me that. After nothing but silence for a whole year, you almost hit me with your car and don't even stop to make sure I'm okay."

They pulled out of the hospital parking lot in silence. Samuel drummed his fingers on the steering wheel as he drove through the streets of town. "I'm sorry about that," he said. "I know it doesn't make it better or right, but I am so sorry. When I saw you driving toward the farm, I panicked a little. I didn't mean to spook your horse. Actually I was going to pull over to talk to you, but then the horse darted, and I took off. I couldn't stand to think that I had done something to harm you like I did to Amos."

The words had just poured out of him, and Sarah sat in stunned silence for a moment. She turned over his apology in her mind, but the thing that she kept coming back to was that he was still blaming himself for Amos' death. She reached out, and took his hand, not saying anything, but just letting him feel her support.

When he turned into a convenience store parking lot, Sarah turned to look at him with a questioning glance. Samuel pulled the car into a spot on the last row, and sat there, his head in his hands.

"This is where it happened," he said. "This is where I let those guys kill my brother."

"You didn't—" Sarah started to say.

"You weren't there," Samuel interrupted. "With all due respect, no one was there but me and Amos and those two....thugs. He was my younger brother, Sarah, I should have been there to protect him, but I was a coward instead. I destroyed my family's whole world. You know how my maemm felt about Amos. He was her golden child. He could do no wrong. I shattered her."

Sarah felt a flash of anger. "Honestly, I think that you destroyed her more with your disappearing act. She didn't just lose one son that day, you know."

"Like I said before," Samuel said, the anguish in his voice clear, "no one else was there so no one else knows what really happened that day."

Sarah sat back in her seat, and stared out the front windshield. *Lord, I need your help again. Please guide me. Tell me what to say to him. He's hurting but only you can fix what needs fixing. Only you can heal his heart. Help me do my part, Lord. Amen.*

Taking a deep breath, Sarah turned to him, and said, "Tell me what happened then."

Part Six:

For a long moment Samuel was so silent, and so still that Sarah worried he might just drive her home, let her out of the car, and drive away forever. She didn't think that her heart could handle such heartbreak. She held her breath.

Samuel opened the door, and gestured for her to get out of the car. Sarah scrambled to follow him as he strode across the parking lot. On the opposite side of the lot, where the parking spaces were closest to the street, Samuel came to a stop. He stepped onto the thin grassy strip dividing the parking lot from the street.

"Amos and I were supposed to deliver the road stand money to the bank, so we came into town with the horse and buggy. I wanted to get the errand done with so that I could get home faster," Samuel began. He stared off into the distance as Sarah watched the memory wash over him. "There was a sing that night, and I wanted to see...well, you."

Sarah flashed him a brief smile, flushing with pleasure at the thought of Samuel wanting to see her all that time ago. She wasn't sure if he could see her smile, but she hoped he knew how much that meant to her.

"But Amos wanted to stop and get some pop and candy before we went on. So we pulled into the parking lot, right here actually. I told Amos that I would stay with the buggy while he ran in to get his stuff," Samuel said as he ran his hands through his hair. Sarah's stomach knotted as she realized what this was leading up to. She wanted to wrap Samuel in a hug and let him know that she was there for him, with him.

"He walked in on an armed robbery," Samuel said. "When he realized what was happening, he turned and ran out of the store. He didn't even make it back to the buggy. The guys chased him out, and shot him in the back. They ran to their getaway car, and I slumped down as far as I could in the seat of the buggy so they wouldn't see me. It wasn't until they were out of the parking lot that I ran to Amos. By then there was a crowd, and someone had called nine-one-one."

"I had no idea, Samuel," Sarah said. It came out lame, but it was all she could think to say. She reached out to take his hand, but he pulled away in anguish.

"Don't you see why I could never go home again? What would my maemm and daed think of me if they knew how I had behaved? How I had just let Amos die?" Samuel sank to his knees, and pressed his face into his hands.

Sarah sank down beside him. "You have no idea how much we all missed you," she said, wrapping her arms around his shoulders.

She held him while the tears came. His shoulders shook, but she held onto him the whole time. Once his sobs had calmed, he wrapped his arms around Sarah, and pressed his face into her shoulder. "I've missed you too."

The two of them clung to each other for a long time, ignoring the cars that whizzed past on the road and the patrons pulling in and out of the convenience store parking lot. Sarah knew that the Lord's hand was working in their lives at that moment. She knew that He had allowed their hearts to crack open, and the time to step toward the future was now.

When they pulled apart, Sarah said, "You don't know the other side of the story. After Amos died, we all felt your absence even more. For me, it felt like half my heart was gone. They don't care about anything other than you coming home. You have to come home, Samuel."

Samuel gazed into her eyes, and Sarah knew that he was hearing her for the first time in a long time. "I don't know if I can," he admitted. "I'm too ashamed."

Sarah took his hand, and still gazing into his eyes, she said, "I'll be right by your side. We'll tell them the story together. Besides, they'll be too happy to have you back, even if you don't believe me."

"Thank you," he said.

"I love you," she replied, surprised at how calm she felt to be making such an admission. "I've always loved you, even when I was angry with you, even when I was missing you."

Samuel shook his head, his eyes shining. "I don't deserve your love," he said. "You are too good for me, but I'm grateful for it. I love you too."

"We should probably get back to the hospital," Sarah said.

Standing, they walked to the car, hand in hand. Sarah glanced over her shoulder. She could picture what he had described, the horror of the scene, his feelings of helplessness. Some other time, she would tell him how glad she was that he had kept himself safe, and how she was certain that Amos would have agreed with her wholeheartedly. It wasn't like Amos to hold a grudge against anyone, he was the most forgiving person she had ever known.

Sarah said as much to Samuel as they started the drive back to the hospital. "I know he forgives you," she said. "Just like Our Father in Heaven has forgiven you. Now you need to forgive yourself."

"I have some mending to do with the Lord before I'll be ready for that," he said, a melancholy note in his voice. "But I'm ready to try to move forward." He paused, and looked over at her. "I can't promise that the process will be fast, but I'd be honored to have you at my side."

"I'll always be at your side from now on," Sarah replied.

"And I'll always thank God for sending me to you today," Samuel said.

"Me too," Sarah agreed. "If you hadn't nearly hit me, you wouldn't have come back into our lives, and you wouldn't have saved your daed."

"The Lord does work in mysterious ways," Samuel agreed as they pulled back into the hospital parking lot.

As they walked back into the hospital, Sarah agreed with what Samuel had said. And even though their future was the biggest mystery of all, she felt certain that with the Lord's help, they would face it together.

The Prideful Amish Girl

Samantha Collier

The notes filled the barn, carrying a tide of joyful singing to the top of the roof.

It was a cold winter's day, and the small Amish community gathered to honour the Lord that Sunday were shivering with the cold.

Linda scratched her neck, trying to turn her collar up against the cold. She looked around her. Mr and Mrs Albrecht's breath was fogging with condensation as they sang. Their two young children were fidgeting with the cold. Mrs Albrecht leaned down to keep them still.

If only someone would close the door, Linda thought. The cold wind was swirling through the barn, and she was afraid that her grandfather might pass out. He was wrapping his coat around himself, swaying slightly. He had suffered a stroke recently, and Linda found herself constantly checking on him ever since.

As if in answer to her silent plea, someone slipped away from the congregation and closed the door. She turned her head slightly. It was Vernon Eicher. She smiled at him, in thank you. He seemed surprised, but smiled tentatively back.

It did the trick. The barn started to warm up, slightly.

Linda closed her eyes, thanking the Lord that the frigid breeze was gone .

The next hymn started. Oh, how she loved this one! She let her voice ring out pure and true, joy enveloping her as she sang. She could feel the eyes of people turning to her, but she didn't care.

When Linda was singing, it was as if the whole world was suspended.

She knew that she had a lovely voice; she had been told often enough. And it wasn't just church service or Evening Sing when she sang. As she did her chores at home, or walked in the woods, she would sing out loud just for the joy of it.

She would practise in her bedroom, standing in front of the mirror. Her mother would tell her off for that, telling her she was being vain. But Linda just thought of it as practise.

It was a communion with God, she knew. God wouldn't have given her such a lovely voice if he hadn't intended her to use it, now would he?

The hymn ended, and so did the service. People started talking, milling around to socialise before lunch.

Linda's best friend, Barbara, made her way to where Linda stood with her family.

"Linda!" she breathed. "You sang so beautifully in that last hymn. The hairs on the back of my neck were standing up. You have the voice of an angel!"

Linda smiled, enjoying the praise. "Thank you, Barbara," she replied. The two young women giggled together.

Afterwards, when everyone sat at the long outdoor tables to enjoy lunch, Linda called Barbara over to sit beside her.

"What do you think of Vernon Eicher?" she whispered to her friend, looking down the table at the young man sitting next to his father. Barbara followed her gaze.

"He is a very solemn young man," Barbara whispered back. "But very handsome! Linda, have you taken a shine to him?"

"Maybe," Linda replied. She stared at Vernon, who felt her gaze and turned her way. She smiled, and she was happy to see that Vernon returned her smile again.

"Linda Heiser."

She turned to see Mrs Albrecht addressing her. The woman was leaning over the table to catch Linda's attention.

"*Ja*, Mrs Albrecht?"

The woman smiled. "I just wanted to say, Linda, how much I admire your singing. You have the most beautiful voice."

Linda preened. She could feel everyone's eyes at the table on her again. She really did love the attention!

"Thank you, Mrs Albrecht," she replied, loudly. "I have practised a lot. But, yes, some people are just born with lovely voices. I think I am one of them."

She heard her mother, who was sitting on the other side of her, gasp.

"My teacher used to say I had the voice of a nightingale," Linda continued. "Old Miss Miller said I could rival the greatest singers of all time!" She puffed out her chest a bit as she spoke.

Her mother nudged her, underneath the table, but Linda ignored her.

"*Ja*, well." Mrs Albrecht's face had frozen slightly. She looked down at her plate.

Linda couldn't resist looking down the table to see if Vernon was listening.

He was. But his face had coloured slightly, and he avoided her eye.

Then she saw the face of his father, old Mr Eicher, staring at her. He was frowning, shaking his head slightly as he did so.

Linda momentarily felt shamed, then she tossed her head back. Who was anybody to comment on what she said about herself?

She had high self-esteem. She always had. She didn't see the point in putting herself down. And when it came to her voice, Linda was proud. She had been told often enough in her life how lovely it was. Why shouldn't she think so, too?

But she had a stab of misgiving when Vernon refused to catch her eye.

***

That night, after she had returned home after the Evening Sing, Linda made her way to her bedroom.

"I want to talk to you, young lady."

She turned around. Her mother, of course. Linda groaned inwardly. Here we go, she thought to herself. Another lecture.

"Linda, why must you persist in being so proud?" Her mother had her hands on her hips and her lips pursed.

Linda kept walking into her room, turning the kerosene lamp on.

She glanced at her mother, sighing. "Do we really have to do this, Mamm? I am tired! It's been a long day." As if to prove her point, she collapsed across the bed, flailing dramatically.

Mrs Heiser frowned. "*Ja*, we really have to do this, daughter of mine." She sat down on the side of the bed. "Linda, we have talked about this a lot. What you did today, at lunch, wasn't acceptable."

Linda looked at her mother. "What did I do?"

Mrs Heiser sighed. "Boasting. You know it was boasting."

Linda sat up, suddenly. "I don't see that it was," she said, crossly. "Mrs Albrecht gave me a compliment. It would have been rude to ignore it."

"There is a difference between taking a compliment," her mother continued, "and turning it into a boast. Saying that your teacher said you had a voice as good as the greatest singers is boasting."

"It's not!" Linda's eyes flashed. "She said it to me! I didn't lie!"

Mrs Heiser stood up. "I will not argue with you," she said. "I want you to pray tonight, and think of what I have said. Our Lord will show you the right way, if you let him." She walked out of the room, closing the door behind her.

Linda sighed again. Why was it always this way?

She knew that her community didn't like people to be prideful. She had been taught that since she was a very young girl.

But it was different when you had a gift, surely? A gift from God? God wanted his children to nurture their talents. That was why he gave them out.

She undressed slowly, praying before she retired.

"Dear Lord," she said, aloud. "Everyone says I am prideful. But why did you gift me with my voice if you didn't want me to be proud of it?

I don't understand." She didn't meditate any further on it. She climbed into bed and turned out the light.

She wouldn't think any more about it. Besides, other things were playing on her mind.

Vernon Eicher. Tonight, he had finally asked her out.

She thought of his dark hair and flashing dark eyes. He was so handsome! The handsomest man in her district. He had courted other girls, never glancing Linda's way. Finally, he had noticed her back. It was a dream come true.

She replayed their conversations over in her head until she finally fell asleep.

***

Vernon arrived shortly after six that Saturday night, ready to take Linda on their date.

Linda was buzzing with excitement, singing as she awaited him.

"Linda! Could you keep it down!" Her brother, Jacob, stuck his head out of the living room door, chiding her.

"Oh, Jacob, why do you always want to spoil my fun?" She twirled around him, laughing.

"Linda! A buggy is here!" Her mother grabbed her, smoothing down her dress as she did so.

Vernon came in, looking especially handsome in his dark suit.

"Where are you young people going tonight?" Her mother looked from one to the other expectantly.

"I am taking Linda to town, Mrs Heiser," Vernon replied. "I thought she might like to look at the Nativity scene in the centre after we have had dinner."

"Lovely," Mrs Heiser replied. "I hope you have a good evening."

"We will, darling Mamm," Linda laughed, kissing her mother on the cheek.

They had a wonderful time in town. Vernon took her to Mast's Diner, where they ate chicken pot pie and butter noodles, followed by a big helping of peach pie. Linda was relieved that conversation was easy, and they had a similar sense of humour, laughing at each other's jokes.

Afterwards, they walked to the town centre, where a beautiful Nativity scene had been set up, complete with life size sheep and the three Wise Kings.

"I always loved looking at Mary, the most," Linda whispered as they stood there. Twinkling lights framed the stable, resembling stars in the night sky.

"She seemed so calm and lovely, in her blue gown and veil, staring down at our Lord." Linda sighed. "Maybe because I always envied calm people. I have always had so much energy, racing from one thing to the next. My mind never stays still." She smiled, a little ruefully.

Vernon looked at her. "That is what I like about you," he said, slowly. "You are always smiling and full of life."

Linda smiled. "That is a lovely thing to say, Vernon," she whispered.

They stared at the Nativity a while longer, soaking in the tranquillity.

That night in bed, Linda could still see the lights twinkling in her head, like lanterns lighting the way to her future.

***

Linda was still dreaming of Vernon over her schapple at the breakfast table the next day.

"Linda!" Her mother nudged her. "Enough day dreaming! You have chores."

Linda nodded. Had she been so obvious?

Did he like her as much as she liked him? She replayed every word and gesture in her head. Yes, she thought. He does like me. But he hadn't suggested another date, an omission which troubled her.

"We have to go into town later, so make sure you have everything finished." Her mother got up, picking up the breakfast dishes as she did.

Linda brightened. They were going into town. That meant that she would be able to make an excuse and slip away to see Vernon. He worked in town, at Eicher's Furniture shop.

Later that day, after they had done their business, Linda turned to her mother.

"I might just go to the bakery," she said. "I could get us some of those cream pies that you like so much and meet you back at the buggy in half an hour?"

She turned and walked away before her mother could say yes or no.

The bakery was on the way to the furniture shop, so she would have enough time to get the cakes and still see Vernon – if he was there, of course.

It was another cold day. Linda turned the collar up on her coat, and put on her mittens. It would be a brisk walk.

The bell tinkled over the door of Eicher's as she entered.

He was here; she could see him in the back, turning the lathe on a table leg. Vernon was a talented furniture maker – her father often said he made the best wooden furniture in the district.

"*Ja?*" The assistant approached her, expectantly.

"Would I be able to go and say hello to Vernon?" She smiled brightly at the woman.

The woman was assessing her, somewhat coldly. "*Ja*, I suppose," she said, slowly. "But please be mindful that he is busy."

Linda walked away, into the back of the shop.

Vernon hadn't seen her, yet. What would he think, of her coming to see him like this? Would he think her too forward?

He looked up at that moment, and saw her. He stopped the lathe slowly.

Her smile wavered slightly. Was he pleased?

He got up, walking toward her. "Linda," he said. "Are you here to buy some furniture?"

She laughed. "Oh, Vernon, you know I can't tell a stool from a chair," she said. "I have just come to say hello." She looked down, feeling a bit awkward. "So, hello."

"Hello," he responded. But he wasn't smiling.

Oh dear. Had she misinterpreted his interest entirely?

"I just wanted to say thank you for a lovely evening," she blurted. "I had a lovely time."

He smiled, then. "I did too," he said. He was gazing at her, as if there was something else he wanted to say.

"Well, I suppose I should go." She looked around her. "You are busy." Ask me out on another date, she thought to herself. Could she will him to do it?

"Would you like to go sledding after work tomorrow?" He looked at her. "There is enough snow on the fields now, I think."

She smiled. "Oh yes!" She looked up at him. "Will you pick me up?"

"*Ja*, be ready around four," he said.

"See you then," she said, walking out of the shop. He did like her! She was grinning widely now. She knew it!

Vernon watched her walk out of the shop. He was deep in thought, and hadn't heard his father approaching.

"Was that the Heiser girl?" Mr Eicher, his father, was standing there, staring disapprovingly at the door.

"It was," Vernon answered, glancing at his father. What would he say?

"You know how I feel about her," Mr Eicher continued. "That girl is too prideful. She doesn't act with the modesty that a young girl should. Always boasting about her singing. You shouldn't court her, Vernon. What about Emma Sommer? She is a modest girl, always respectful."

"I don't really like Emma," Vernon said. He looked at his father. "But I do like Linda. I know what you mean about her boasting – she can be prideful. But could I talk to her about it, see if I can get her to see how pride is wrong?"

Mr Eicher frowned. "I don't know, Vernon. In my experience, people don't change much."

"Please, Daed?"

Mr Eicher looked at his son. "You really do like her, don't you?" He scratched his head. "Alright, I will let you court her, for now. But I don't really see any future in it. I will give you two months to prove that she is worthy of you." He turned to go. "You should really think about courting a girl like Emma – they are the ones that make good wives, my son."

He walked away. Vernon stared after him for a while, then slowly turned back to the lathe.

Linda. She was so full of life, smiling and chatting. She was like a breath of fresh air. He had liked her for a while, but hadn't had the courage to approach her. He had enjoyed their date. But he had been unsure since – he knew that his father didn't approve of her.

He understood what his father meant about her. She did boast, and seemed unaware that she was doing it – or if she was aware, she didn't care. But she could change, couldn't she?

Vernon stared thoughtfully at the lathe.

He would have to have a talk with her about it, if he wanted to keep seeing her.

But how would she take it?

***

They laughed in the snow, throwing snowballs at each other, breathless.

Vernon stared at Linda as she ran, throwing snow behind her. Her face was aglow, and her dark hair was escaping her *kapps*. He didn't think he had ever seen a more vibrant girl. She really was like a light in the darkness.

Afterwards, over a hot chocolate at her kitchen table, they laughed.

He took her hand, lifting it to his mouth, and kissed it.

Linda gasped. Tremors ran through her, starting from the spot where Vernon had kissed her hand all the way to the soles of her feet.

He looked at her. The gaze seemed to go on forever.

"Linda." He stopped, as if he was unsure how to continue.

"*Ja?*" she breathed. She couldn't believe how blue his eyes were. They were the color of a cornflower, waving in the breeze on a hot summer's day.

"I like you, you know that." He looked uncomfortable. "I like you a lot. I want to keep courting you. But there is something that I need to talk to you about."

"What is it?" She picked up her hot chocolate and took a sip, surprised to see her hands were shaking slightly.

"It's the way you boast." He shifted in the chair. "Everyone says it about you. About how you boast about your singing."

Linda felt the hairs on the back of her neck start to bristle. "That is their opinion," she said. "Why should I let the small minds of other people effect the way that I feel about myself?"

She looked at him. "You don't care about such silliness, do you?"

Vernon sighed. "Like I said, I like you a lot," he said. "More and more every time we are together. But it does worry me. You were very loud and boastful when Mrs Albrecht complimented you after the Service last Sunday. People notice, and talk. I think you should just tone it down a little, that's all."

She felt her face reddening. "Do you think I have a lovely voice?"

"*Ja*, but..."

"But nothing." She stood up, gathering the cups. "It is known. I'm not making it up – I have been told forever how lovely my voice is. Why should I deny it, just because a few small minded people have a problem with how I talk?"

"But, Linda…"

"I think you should go, now." She turned away from him.

He sighed deeply, but picked up his hat and stood to leave.

"If that's how you feel," he said.

"That's how I feel."

He turned and walked toward the door. "Can I see you again?"

She looked at him, then softened. "Of course, Vernon. You know how much I like you."

"Shake my hand, then," he said, offering his own.

She walked toward him, putting her hand in his.

They both gasped at the electric current which sparked between them.

Vernon sat in the buggy to collect his thoughts before he left the Heiser's farm.

She wasn't interested in talking about it. She had bristled as soon as he had brought it up.

Which was a real problem.

He knew now that he loved her, and wanted her to be his wife.

But how could he convince his father?

***

Linda set the table for dinner that night, deep in thought.

Vernon. He was the sweetest, gentlest man she had ever met. Kind, polite, respectful…and his touch electrified her in a way that she had never dreamt possible. Was this love?

But what about what he had said to her? That she boasted too much? How could she think seriously about a man who thought that she was flippant and vain?

Linda knew that she was forward, and spoke her mind. She knew that the elders, especially, thought her not meek enough.

But she was who she was – how could she change that, for anyone? Even if it was for Vernon.

"Let us pray." The family sat down for dinner, her father at the head of the table.

She dropped her head, as they prayed silently before their meal.

She usually rushed through it, eager to think of other things, or wolf down the meal in front of her.

But tonight, she closed her eyes and formulated her prayer.

Dear Lord, Thank you for the meal that we are about to eat. I am grateful for this bounty, and for my family sitting here, safe and well.

She frowned slightly, then thought more.

Thank you for Vernon, and the relationship that I feel developing between us. He is such a good man, Lord. I want to please him and be the best woman that I can for him.

But Lord, how do I stop being myself? If he wants me, shouldn't he accept the way that I am? How can I change for him? But most importantly, Lord – do you want me to?

She still had her eyes closed as the family slowly picked up their utensils and started eating.

"Linda?"

Her mother's soft voice roused her. She shook her head, then slowly picked up her knife and fork.

Mrs Heiser looked at her daughter. Linda was in an unusually pensive mood tonight. It wasn't like her rambunctious daughter to get lost in contemplation, especially at the dinner table.

What was happening with her? Whatever it was, Mrs Heiser thought it was transforming her – for the better.

***

Christmas had come and gone, and New Year was upon them.

Linda stared out the window, at the snow blanketing the terrain. She couldn't believe sometimes how much things had changed.

She and Vernon were officially an item.

He wasn't the type of man she had expected to find herself with.

He was solemn, and thought before he spoke. He was slow to smile and laugh, but when he did, his joy was fulsome. He was in every way the polar opposite of her – she, who was so quick to act, and left thinking to afterwards.

But she thought that they complemented each other well. She gave him energy when his flagged. And he gave her fresh perspective, a new approach to life. She admired his hard work and discipline – she was usually so flighty, she had to force herself to be still.

But there was one thing that troubled her.

He hadn't mentioned love or marriage, or even spoke as if they had a permanent future together.

She remembered the look on his face after the Christmas singing at the local nursing home.

He had joined her, although he usually didn't. Their choir numbered about ten, and was usually the same people from year to year.

The old people had sat in the lounge of the home, blankets over their laps, gazing expectantly. The group had rehearsed for a few weeks prior, and had their set list of favorites, such as *Silent Night* and *Away In A Manger.*

It had started well. Vernon had led the prayer prior, and then they had started singing, moving rapidly through their repertoire.

The old people had loved it, singing along with them and clapping their hands. She had noticed an old lady at the front, who whispered to one of the staff when their set was over. The nurse had approached her.

"Gladys wants to know if you could sing a carol by yourself. She said you have such a beautiful voice, she would love to hear you," the nurse had said.

Linda could see Vernon frowning, shaking his head no. But she couldn't disappoint an old lady, could she?

"I'd be delighted," she said.

She started singing *Angels We Have Heard On High*, one of her favorites that hadn't made the main list this year. She could hear the gasps of appreciation from the old people, and they clapped thunderingly when she finished.

She bowed, glowing with happiness. She felt like she was on cloud nine, as if her feet couldn't touch the ground.

But when she looked back at Vernon, his face was dark.

In the buggy on the way home that night, he didn't speak to her. They pulled up at her house, and she climbed down, waiting for him to say something.

"Vernon, are you angry with me?" Her voice was tremulous.

He gazed to the front, not looking at her. "I wonder that you want to make a spectacle of yourself."

She blanched. "The old lady asked me to sing!" She tried to swallow the lump that had formed in her throat. "It would have been discourteous to refuse."

"But why do you have to take such pleasure in it? Being the centre of attention, like a bird preening its feathers?"

She felt tears pricking behind her eyes. "You don't understand," she said. How could she explain it? "It comes through me. It is like a gift that I feel that I am giving to the world. It feels holy, like God commands it. Don't you have anything that you feel that way about? What about your wood work – you are so talented at it! Don't you feel that you would be denying the world something if you didn't work with your hands, making that beautiful furniture?"

He slowly looked at her. "I do like wood work," he whispered. "I do feel holy in its pursuit. *Ja,* I do understand what you mean when you say that."

She swallowed. "I am trying, Vernon," she said. "But it is hard. I am who I am. Why can't you accept me?"

He stared at her. "I am sorry to pain you, Linda. I know you are trying." He looked away. How could he explain his father's conditions? That she must show that she was becoming less vain about her voice?

She wouldn't understand. She thought that taking pride in her voice was as natural as breathing.

Vernon frowned. She was like a peacock, showy with her beautiful feathers. But the peacock had just as much right to exist as the less showy sparrow, didn't it? Just because one was different to the other, didn't make either of them wrong.

It was becoming too hard. "I will speak to you, soon." He picked up the reins, spurring the horses on into the night.

Linda had stared after him, until he was a pin prick in the distance.

She thought of it now, as she stared out the window. Would he ever learn to accept her, the way that she was? Or would he be forever trying to change her?

***

He asked to speak to her, alone, the very next night.

She couldn't help but feel a small flicker of excitement. Was this going to be it? Was he going to propose to her?

But she was ambivalent. The better part of her longed for him, would walk to the ends of the earth to be his wife. The worst part of her was resentful at his insistence that she change who she was. What would be her answer, if he did ask her?

He walked into the house, taking off his hat, stamping his feet on the door mat to get rid of snow clinging to his pants.

Her mother greeted him, then made a discreet exit. Linda thought that her mother probably thought that this was going to be a proposal, too.

They sat down at the kitchen table, after Linda had poured them both a coffee. He stared at his cup for a long, long time before he looked at her.

"Linda…" His voice trailed off. He swallowed awkwardly.

"*Ja?*" She smiled, tentatively.

"It's like this." He swallowed again. "My father has put a condition on me courting you. He says that you must change; show that you are not boasting anymore, before he will agree to me putting a proposal of marriage to you." He looked down at his coffee cup again.

"What?" Linda thought that she had misheard. Mr Eicher was dictating that she had to change?

Then it hit her, right in the solar plexus. It felt like she was back in the school yard, when Jebediah King had pushed her so hard she had hit the ground, winded.

"Linda, it is possible." He reached out for her hand, picking it up. She didn't resist. "You just have to tone it down a little. Pretend you are Emma Sommer."

"Pretend I am Emma Sommer?" she repeated, looking down at her hand in his.

"Well, I didn't mean that exactly, of course." He let her hand go, running his own through his hair. This wasn't going exactly as he wanted it to. "I mean, try to act like her a little – you know how meek she is, barely saying boo to anyone. Blushing when anyone says anything to her. Then my father might agree to us marrying."

"You want me to act like Emma Sommer?" she repeated. "So that your father will agree to us marrying?"

"*Ja,*" he nodded. Did she understand him, after all? He looked at her, ready to smile.

But Linda wasn't smiling. In fact, he had rarely seen her so angry. She stood up.

"You can tell your father," she said, carefully, "that I have no intention of changing for anyone. And as far as us marrying goes – well, Vernon Eicher, I wouldn't marry you if you were the last man on earth!"

He paled. "What?" he stammered.

"You heard me," she continued. "The front of you! You haven't even asked *me*, Vernon, if I want to marry you, before you ask *your father*?" She shook her head. "You presume too much! I don't care to discuss it at all! I would like you to leave, now."

Vernon stood up. He was shaking. "Linda…"

"No," she said. She didn't look at him, picking up his hat and giving it to him. "Good bye, Vernon."

"Oh, and one more thing," she said. "You can tell your father that I wouldn't want to be Emma Sommer in my wildest dreams."

She pushed him out of the door, then leaned against it, breathing heavily.

The tears when they came were hot and salty. It felt good to release them.

***

Mrs Heiser looked at her daughter. This was the second day now that Linda had slept in, claiming that she was coming down with a cold.

She knew her daughter, knew that a mere cold couldn't shake that indomitable energy.

But something had. And she would bet that something had a name: Vernon Eicher.

"So what happened between you and Vernon?" she said, from the doorway.

Linda glanced at her mother, pulling the blankets higher. "Nothing."

Mrs Heiser sighed. "Linda, it's obvious. You have been in a black mood ever since he left on Tuesday night."

Linda sat up suddenly. "He wants me to be Emma Sommer!"

"What?" Mrs Heiser wasn't expecting that. "The Sommers from the next town's youngest girl? What on earth are you talking about?"

Linda laughed suddenly, a bit hysterically. "I am not good enough for his father, apparently. They both want me to act like Emma

Sommer, if not actually *be* her. Why doesn't Vernon just court her instead? Then he, his father and Emma can all ride off into the sunset together, happy as larks!"

"Linda," her mother scolded.

Linda's bottom lip trembled, and she burst into tears.

Her mother came toward her, putting her arms around her. "Hush, now," she said, crooning. "It will be all right. Take a deep breath and calm yourself."

Linda took a deep breath, but the tears kept coming. "He doesn't love me, Mamm. Not for who I am."

"What does he say?" her mother asked, gently.

"He says that I boast too much about my voice," she said. "His father thinks that I am full of pride, and wants me to change before he will give his stamp of approval to Vernon to ask for my hand in marriage."

Mrs Heiser sighed. "That is hard, Linda." She paused, looking at her daughter. "How does Vernon feel about that?"

"I don't know," Linda replied. "He has often said that he thinks me too boastful, but he hasn't mentioned his father before. He was mad at me for singing solo at the nursing home at Christmas. Said that I should have refused, that I was taking pride in being asked to sing by myself."

"Well," said Mrs Heiser, "that would be hard for Vernon – having his father put conditions on his courtship with you. Vernon must be torn. I have observed him with you, Linda, and he really does have a great respect for you."

Linda's eyes softened. "Do you think so? Why does he want to change me, then?"

"I don't think he is trying to change you, not really," her mother responded. "He has asked you to tone things down, not to boast. Is that so hard? Maybe he shouldn't have got mad at you for singing solo, not when you were asked specifically. It would have been rude to refuse

– and besides, it gave joy to those poor old people in that home at Christmas. He has confused it, a bit. But then he is under pressure from his father."

Linda nodded, slowly. "I think I understand, a little. At least, I understand how hard it must be for Vernon."

Her mother kissed her, standing up. "I want you to do something for me," she said. "I want you to study your bible tonight. Really study it. Try to see the truth in what Vernon asks you – for it is the truth, my *lieb*. You boast, and we have spoken about it many times. I want you to reflect on the difference between boasting and taking pride in a job well done."

Linda looked up at her mother, and nodded. "All right, Mamm. I will try."

"Good girl," her mother said, ruffling her hair. Then she left.

Linda stared down at her bible on the bedside table.

She would get up, do her chores, and she would study it tonight, just like her mother asked her to.

***

She sat down at her dressing table that night, lit her lantern and opened it up.

Her mother had directed her to some passages.

The first was Proverbs 27:2, which stated, "Let another praise you, and not your own mouth; a stranger, and not your own lips." She sat back and thought.

The quote was saying that people could praise you, but that you shouldn't praise yourself. It wasn't saying that your gift, or skill, or talent, couldn't exist in the world for other people to enjoy.

Perhaps that was what she had always been fearful of: that if she admitted that she boasted and that it was wrong, it would mean she mustn't share her gift with the world. That scared her. She felt she must sing like she must breathe. It was essential to her nature.

Then she read Psalms 10:4, which stated that people who are proud are so consumed with themselves that their thoughts weren't with God. That pride got in the way of real communion with Him.

She could see the truth in that. When she was boasting, her thoughts weren't with God; she was self-absorbed, basking in her own glory. She thought of the difference between her thrill at seeing the old people react with such joy at her singing, to her feeling of smugness when someone told her how lovely her voice was, or when she boasted about it. There was a world of difference: one was satisfaction at giving joy, the other was pride. Pure and simple.

Linda closed the book, deep in thought. She must talk to Vernon.

There were things they must discuss. She must try to bridge the gap that had sprung up between them.

***

He came around the next day, as she requested.

Her family were absent, had made themselves busy doing other things. She inwardly thanked them; it was essential that they had privacy.

He sat down at the table. She had made a fresh pot of coffee and a cinnamon coffee cake, which was still hot from the oven.

"Would you like a slice?" she asked. He nodded, in silence.

It was awkward, there was no doubt about that. She tried to smile, but it emerged a bit lopsided.

He picked up his fork, and took a bite. "It's good," he said.

She was about to say that of course it was, it was her grandmother's famous recipe, then she stopped herself. Her grandmother wouldn't have said that. Her grandmother would have nodded, remarked that she was glad he enjoyed it, and left it at that.

So that's exactly what Linda did.

It felt good; lighter, somehow. He picked up his coffee cup, and watched her.

"Vernon," she said. "I asked you here because I wanted to apologise."

His eyebrows raised. He wasn't used to Linda saying sorry for anything.

"I think I finally understand," she continued. "What you were saying, about being boastful. I have thought a lot about it." She stopped, looking at him. He nodded encouragement.

"I was scared," she admitted. "Scared that if I accepted what everyone told me, I wouldn't be able to sing anymore. That I was saying it was wrong to do so. But that's not what you mean, is it?"

"Of course not," he said. "I have never said you aren't able to sing."

"It felt that way, after the nursing home," she said, lowering her eyes.

He reddened. "It came out all wrong," he said. "I know it sounded like I was saying that you shouldn't have sung. But you were right, then. It gave such joy to the people it would have been wrong to deny them. I was just frustrated. I was under pressure from my father."

"I know," she said. "It must have been hard."

He looked at her. "Very hard," he said. He groped for his words. "I'm sorry about the other day. I don't want you to be Emma Sommer! I like you, Linda. In fact..." he paused, reddening. "I love you."

She gasped. "Oh, Vernon. I love you, too."

He stood up, overwhelmed. "I have been longing to tell you, for so long! But I didn't want to mention it, in case my father stood in our way."

"I know you are right, now," she said. "I will never boast again. I understand how it makes me appear to others, and how wrong it is to be so self-absorbed."

He looked at her, his eyes shining. "If I can speak to my father and get his approval, will you consent to be my wife?"

She flung her arms around him. "Oh, yes, Vernon. Yes, please!"

They kissed, tenderly.

"I am going, this minute," he said, grabbing his hat. "I have to speak to him." He kissed her, again, and then was off.

She stared at him through the window.

Vernon loved her. She loved Vernon. Hopefully, she would be his wife, soon.

If Mr Eicher would allow it.

***

Vernon came back later that day, with shining eyes.

"I spoke to my father," he said. "He is allowing it! I explained our conversations, and how you finally understand about pride. He is satisfied." He beamed at her.

"So we can be married?" she breathed.

"If you'll have me," he responded, suddenly shy.

"I would walk the ends of the earth to be your wife," she said, simply.

They embraced.

It was true – she loved him for eternity.

She was the luckiest woman in the world. And she would never boast again.

An Amish Widow's Window

110

Amanda Roxley

Chapter 1: Flashbacks

Falling in love can happen all at once and also over a long period of time. Some people say that there is only one moment, and in that moment, you know that you've fallen in love. Falling in love, for Elizabeth, happened more or less, by accident. Elizabeth Brenneman fell in love suddenly yet slowly at the same time. His name was James Harper. She was sitting inside the Neptune Diner on the corner of Pine and Orange Streets with some of her new English girlfriends when James Harper arrived on the scene. James was the boyfriend of Megan Sanchez, a short plumpy Latino girl, with thick dark brown girls. She was also endowed with a generous chest, an amazing smile, and a silly laugh. When James came to the diner at 1 am in the morning and sat down by Megan, Elizabeth liked him immediately, but never thought she would fall in love with James. Why?

♦ James was Megan's boyfriend,

♦ James was an Englishman.

♦ She was/is(?) Amish.

♦ Elizabeth was an honest girl.

♦ James was wrong for Elizabeth in every way.

♦ James had a huge tattoo on his left shoulder (and Elizabeth didn't care for the Englishmen's tattoos.)

Elizabeth loved the Lord, and she never wanted to fall into a path that led to dishonesty, cheating, or leaving her family. She didn't cheat, actually, but it felt like it. While Elizabeth was experiencing Rumspringa, a time when Amish youth are allowed to enter the "modern world" and decide if they want to remain Amish, she found herself taking a liking to the English dance styles. Every Friday night

Elizabeth and her new English friends would go to a local Christian church hall and take part in something called contra dancing. Contra dancing occurred in a square formation, but you also danced with your partner and up and down the hall in lines with another set of partners simultaneously. In fact, it was quite difficult to explain what contra was or why she loved it, but she did, nonetheless. Elizabeth wasn't quite used to dancing with so many people, but it was fun, and she loved the music. There was an array of sounds that filled the air; delicate, yet elaborate wooden instruments with strings produced a sound that she had never heard before. The people dressed in long, flowy skirts, in bright oranges, blues, pinks, and even reds, as they danced across the hall with a grace that she longed to achieve.

Although Elizabeth usually arrived without a date to the local Friday night contra dancing, one night Megan said she could not go dancing and it wasn't a problem if she went with James. Elizabeth considered what a quandary that put her in...if she was in her Amish community this would never happen. Of course, a lot of things would never happen, such as dancing, going out on a Friday night, or drinking a milkshake at 1 am at the local diner. She loved all of it and hated all of it at the same time because Rumspringa showed her a whole new world, but that world did not include her family, and it did include James and Meg.

From the night that Elizabeth and James danced together, Elizabeth felt a spark in her heart that no Amish man had ever given her. She felt the feeling of being light on her feet, a feeling that could hardly be described with words. When he smiled at her nothing could keep a smile off her face. Since the evening that Elizabeth and James danced together, the two kept their feelings under lock and key regarding their unspoken attraction. Megan, however, saw that James was into Elizabeth and perhaps Elizabeth was interested in James too, so she broke-up with James even though she liked him. In some strange way, Megan gave them her blessing and saw their relationship all the way to the altar.

Even as Elizabeth uttered the words, "I do, she felt her heart break in two. Her life forever was divided. Her heart, well, was even more so divided. Her decision to wed James came with the decision to leave her family. Now, she found herself even more torn and heartbroken, because she was without James. She received the phone call when she was sitting at home sewing little booties for their baby on the way. James' boss, Marshall Hoover, called from the bar, where James worked as a bartender. Marshall started speaking slowly in a hushed tone. That was when Elizabeth knew that something was wrong. Elizabeth always knew Marshall, in the short time she had known him, to be a man who spoke his mind, and didn't hold back.

The conversation came back to Elizabeth in pieces. She still couldn't remember all of it. There had been an accident... James wasn't feeling very well when he came into work.... James looked pale... he was pouring drinks... and then he collapsed on the floor. A bar patron called 911, but by the time the ambulance arrived he was already gone. Elizabeth kept running the phone call through her head as if somehow it would change things or bring James back. James had suffered a fatal heart attack. They didn't know that James had a heart condition, but apparently, he did. He was too young to die. She was too young to be a widow. But she was. Elizabeth Brenneman was a widow.

Chapter 2: Not the Only Broken Heart

Elizabeth Brenneman was not the only one with a broken heart. More than one fellow yearned to marry Elizabeth Brenneman and was devastated when Elizabeth unexpectedly fell in love on Rumspringa. Elizabeth was the kind of girl you knew would be a loving, caring wife, and a sweet and tender mother. Any young Amish boy would dream of being Elizabeth's husband up until the point when Elizabeth left the community for James. Although the Amish community agreed that it was too bad that Elizabeth's husband had died so suddenly and at such a young age, there were not so many suitors that were still in interested in Elizabeth. Who would want to marry a young pregnant widow with a baby on the way?

Elizabeth did not feel the need to marry again, but she did feel the fear of raising her baby boy alone. Three weeks after James died, she found herself at Lancaster Women and Babies' Hospital. She was pushing, pushing, with only Megan by her side. Megan remained dedicated to Elizabeth, out of love and also of a sense of duty, because she allowed and even encouraged Elizabeth to date James. Little did she know she would be next to Elizabeth's side without James, as she birthed her child. After James Brenneman was born, Elizabeth found herself unable to care for her own child. She felt that giving her boy, his father's name would give him a sense of pride one day, but she also wanted to honor her Amish heritage and gave her boy her own last name.

The problem with giving birth and grieving a dead husband at the same time was that it was simply impossible. James looked like his father which made it harder and easier at the same time. James Junior had a round face, with olive skin and a small tuft of dark brown hair on the top of his head. He made everyone smile and laugh, and even though Elizabeth was eligible to receive financial support from the government she did not want to raise her boy in the English word without his father. She chose to leave her home for her husband, but without her husband, Elizabeth suffered. Whatever glow James put in her step was taken away by his death. There was only one true option, returning home, destined to remain a widow for the rest of her life.

She feared the reaction of her parents who were naturally crushed when she told them she fell in love and wanted to marry an Englishmen. When her husband died that night in the bar serving drinks she couldn't even think to tell her parents. Her father rejected her when she left and couldn't handle the thought of Elizabeth leaving the family, her home, their home, the community. It took Elizabeth over a month after his death to send a message to her parents through a friend that he passed away. She never heard a response from her parents and assumed that they did not want anything to do with her again. That was certainly more than fair considering what she had done. Sometimes she wondered if God was punishing her for marrying James? Wasn't God a good God? A fair God? A just God? A loving God? Surely the God that she learned about from her family and her community would not want her to be like this. To be broken hearted and alone. She would return. She would go back and then what? Only God knew.

Chapter 3: Strange English Ways

There was a community meeting to decide the fate of the young and no longer naïve Elizabeth and her newborn son, James. Her parents seemed to be unable to face her return as it would bring shame to their family, and her former friends and neighbors did not want to say anything against the Brenneman family for fear that they would lose even their respect. In a strange way, even though the Brennnemans did not want to respect the request of their daughter to return with her son, nobody wanted to speak in favor of Elizabeth, except one, Wayne Bender.

Wayne Bender was not an important man in the community, but he was a male voice, and in the Amish community, elders and men received the most respect. Wayne had a strong, solid, sounding voice that echoed through the hall. "Do we not preach forgiveness? Do we not believe in giving the homeless a home? Do we not believe in clothing the naked? Do we not believe in caring for the sick?" asked Wayne. The Beatitudes were what Wayne preached. "How could we call ourselves the children of God if we turn against one of our own in her time of need? Can we deny the needs of her newborn son?" roared Wayne through the town hall.

There were murmurs among the people until one by one the townspeople agreed with Wayne. How could they forsake Elizabeth?

Even though her own parents were not quick to forgive, for certain, she was in her hour of need, as was her son. With Wayne's words, the community softened and agreed that something could be done. Finally, one of the elderly women in the community, Mary, stood up and spoke on her behalf. "Elizabeth and her boy can live in my spare shed that I'm not using anymore. It's not really a fit living space, but I hate to see a girl on the street with a little one. I would need some help to make it a livable area, a bed for the girl, a crib for the little boy, and a proper toilet and sink. I suppose it could really use a new coat of paint and the windows are a little loose too. They make an awful rattling sound in the wind," she stated.

Slowly others chimed in. "Mary, if you have the space, I can help you with the labor," said Mary's son, Solomon. Wayne immediately agreed that he could help with renovations too. Slowly, but surely, the voices of those wanting to help Elizabeth were much greater than those who remained silent or in objection. "Actually, my husband knows plumbing, I bet he can connect a toilet outdoors," said another neighbor. So, it was decided that they would accept the return of Elizabeth and her son, despite the situation being extremely unusual, and the fact that typically those who chose to leave the Amish community were never permitted to return.

Meanwhile, Elizabeth sat with her son James in her and her former husband's apartment in shock. As tears rolled down her cheek she caressed her sweet son's face. Everything about James reminded her of her husband. How could it be possible that God allowed her to be in this position? If God was so loving then why did bad things happen to good people? She saw so much of her husband was in her young son including his pleasant demeanor. The one thing that Elizabeth had to be thankful for was her son's never-ending smiles and his ability to sleep through the night. She started attending a widow's support group in the city, but went only twice, after she realized that all the attendees were at least over the age of 60, and Elizabeth was barely

22. The moderator of the support group, a soft-spoken elderly woman, Josefine Reagan, caught Elizabeth on the way out the door the second and last time she attended the group.

"My dear, I know you are hurting, I wish there was something I could do for you, and I see that you are struggling. I know this group, well... we just aren't quite your age group, but you're welcome to go to Water Street Rescue Mission. There they help a lot of people in need. They have even depression support groups and single mother's groups. I hope I'm not offending you my dear, and of course you're still more than welcome to come here, but I think there you might find what you are looking for," said Josefine, as she handed Elizabeth a pamphlet with the address and phone number of the Water Street Rescue Mission on it.

"Thanks, I appreciate it really, said Elizabeth as tears rolled down her face. Despite trying to control her emotions she couldn't help but feel everything. Why did she have to feel everything? Everything. Everything was okay before Rumspringa. She began to feel an anger building up inside her, a feeling that she was not used to experiencing. Anger. It's just a stage of grief. That's what the therapist at the hospital had told her after James had passed away. The therapist, much like everyone else, handed her a card with her phone number on it and offered support, but whatever support the modern English word could offer could not compare with what support her home community would offer her if they accepted her back.

Elizabeth almost forgot that she was still standing in front of Josefine due to her scattered thoughts. She bid her goodbye and gave her an awkward half-hug before walking away. She did not turn around or even look at the woman's eyes. Josefine was doing the best she could, but Elizabeth knew already the support group was not going to be able to help her in any way. These women wanted to sit and sew and spew out good memories of all the years they spent with their husbands, of what their grown adult-age children were doing now, and how they enjoyed still being a part of the church, singing in the choir, cleaning the pews and dusting the statues.

While listening to the English widows speak, she longed for her own church community and a proper upbringing for her son. As she reached her apartment door she knew she was already resolved to return if they would have her back. She crumpled up the Water Street Rescue Mission pamphlet with her right hand and threw it on the ground as she turned the key to her apartment with her left hand. She wondered if her little boy would be left-handed like herself or right-handed like her father. Amidst her thoughts, she decided that even though her parents never returned her message but she would go, nonetheless.

Chapter 4: Healing Takes a Lifetime

Megan and Elizabeth sat together in the same diner where Elizabeth first met James, each drinking a coffee. Megan wanted Elizabeth to remember something special and at least their friendship. As a gesture of their friendship and where they came from, Megan asked Elizabeth to come out of her apartment and meet her one last time at the diner for "old time's sake." Elizabeth brought little James Junior in tow on her back. Elizabeth ordered her favorite breakfast for dinner, something that would typically never be allowed in her community. This was, after all, supposed to be a celebration of friendship. Not everything could be gray skies and tears forever.

Crispy hash browns, a Belgian waffle smothered a butter and sugary syrup, four slices of beef bacon, and a glass of apple juice. For certain this meal was a sin, but they were all of Elizabeth's favorite English breakfast foods. She had never seen so many carbohydrates that tasted so good yet so different from the flavors of home. She could not imagine her mother connecting electricity to the house, let alone using a waffle iron like the ones they used in the diner. For a few moments, Elizabeth found her laughing and smiling with Meg and baby James.

Meg asked Elizabeth, "Do you remember when I brought James to the diner, and you met him for the first time?" "How could I forget?" asked Elizabeth, somewhat happy and somewhat sad to be reminded of her dead husband. "You know girl, if you were anybody else, I would have called you a boyfriend stealer!" shouted Meg, a little louder than necessary. The waitress glared at Meg a little but none of the customers raised their heads even a little or dared to look at the two girls and the baby at the table by the window, creating more noise than usual. Their usual waitress was absent and she would never have said a thing, as she knew everything, well... almost everything about their lives. Regardless, Elizabeth attempted to shush Meg, which made the two only laugh louder. Not to mention that milk squirted through Meg's noise and went all over the table.

After an hour or so Elizabeth found herself reminded of her new responsibilities and her new life. "Meg, really, thank you so much, for everything, I mean it, but you know I have to go back," said Elizabeth. "I know," said Meg. "I love you, really, but James and I... we need a family. We are a family, but we have to go back. It's time for this little kiddo to meet his grandparents. I hope they want to meet us," stated Elizabeth. "You know girl, you got some courage!" said Meg. "Let's hit the road, shall we?" asked Elizabeth. "Damn, girl, you are practically an 'English lady' already. You and your non-Amish phrases like, 'let's hit the road.' I'm gonna miss you toots!" pronounced Meg.

As the two left the room, Elizabeth glanced around the diner, took mental snapshots in her mind of the room, her friendship with Meg, and even the food. She looked down at baby James, cooed him to sleep, and the two took off in the car for one last ride in the country together. Although they hoped it wouldn't be the last, they had to be a bit realistic. The wind wiped in circles around their bodies. Meg felt the time slipping away as the sun dipped below the horizon. Reds mixed with oranges colored the sky. Tall corn stalks dotted the countryside and the radio played Sia's "*No Cheap Thrills,*" as they curved around Lancaster County's corners. For a moment, just a moment, Elizabeth laughed a true laugh.

Chapter 5: Whatever Shall Come, Will Come

Wayne stood in front of Mary's shed and considered all the work that would need to be done in order to make it livable for a young mother like Elizabeth. It certainly wasn't a palace, but it could be home with the help of the community. In the end, about 60% of the community had agreed to pitch in materials and labor to make the shed a home for Elizabeth and James Junior. Elizabeth's parents, however, remained silent on the matter, as they suffered from their own struggle of having felt rejected from their daughter when she chose to marry an Englishman. After all, who could blame them for having more than mixed feelings about their daughter's expected return? Although Elizabeth had not explicitly stated that she would return it was understood by her message to her parents that this was the best possible outcome for her and her newborn.

While Elizabeth struggled with the thought of raising James alone and the possible innumerable number of reactions her parents could have to her request to returning to the community, Wayne assembled a building crew. Wayne gathered some of the community's best painters, plumbers, wood workers, and gardeners. Fortunately for Elizabeth, it was the growing season and if seeds were planted now Elizabeth would at least have a wide array of fruits and vegetables ready for her to eat in the summer, and she could freeze anything she could not eat.

One of the best things about the Amish community was how they stood together in solidarity. As Elizabeth was packing her bags and negotiating the remaining payment on the lease with her landlord, Wayne and his assembled team added an extra small room to the shed. They knocked out a wall and created a bedroom for Elizabeth and her son. In the main "room" someone had donated a wood-burning stove and another community member donated an armchair. Quickly the additional room was added to the shed, which was to be Elizabeth's new home. Behind the shed, a few of the woman worked the land, turned the soil, and planted seeds so that Elizabeth could have an abundance of food in a few months. A plumber installed an outdoor toilet in an adjacent building, and within the day the space looked like someone could actually like there. It was no longer just a place for sheep, ox, and or even a working man's tools. It was a home.

Wayne, however, had another interest in helping Elizabeth, besides his altruistic reason. Since he was no more than 15 he had his eyes on Elizabeth. Never, never, in a thousand years could he have imagined that Elizabeth would fall in love with an Englishman while on Rumspringa, nor, could he believe that perhaps he was getting his second chance to be with Elizabeth. He desired so much to be with her and also to be a father. Someone needed to be a father to the little boy, and even if she would not have her, James needed a man in his life to teach him about life and to show him the ways of the world, not just the Amish world, but also even the English world. He should be able to make his own decision one day about whether or not he wanted to return to the English world of his father or stay Amish. Undoubtedly, Elizabeth would want her son to be baptized in the church when she returned.

Wayne was counting on her returning. How would he explain to the community that they had prepared a place for her and her newborn to live if she never came back? Wayne resolved that, as per Amish custom, all things had to be determined with a calm mind and a steady fist. Since he had neither of those at the moment, he made his way to his father's house to see if he was okay. Ever since his mother died, his father struggled to feel himself. Even though he always appeared to be himself to the public, he knew that on the inside he struggled.

The night air was thin, the stars shined more brightly than the previous nights as there was not a cloud in sight. He remembered a multitude of nights from when he was a boy that he longed to view the stars, but the sky remained covered in clouds and blocked his beautiful view. The city of Lancaster, albeit, not a very large one, compared to other English cities, still also created light pollution that sometimes also affected his ability to see the stars. Tonight, however, was simply perfect. The stars were aligned in the sky and brightly lit as if the stars knew his deepest desires.

Chapter 6: The Birth of a New Day

Aside from a few sentimental items and several English gadgets that Elizabeth decided to keep, she more or less abandoned her English life. Her husband's watch and wedding ring, several English novels, fine china that was a wedding gift from Meg, wedding photos, English drink mix called Kool-Aid, and a roll of duct tape all made her suitcases but what Elizabeth could not carry in her suitcase she left to Meg. A return to her roots, to simplicity, was what she and James needed now if they were going to be okay.

As Elizabeth approached the home of her Aunt Abigail with baby James and her few belongings she felt herself shake inside with fear. She knocked lightly on the door and was relieved when her Aunt Abigail was overjoyed to see her return. "Oh, my dear, Elizabeth. I'm so sorry, I could not believe when I heard the news. This must be James Junior. What a sweet little boy you have, Liz," pronounced Elizabeth's aunt. "Oh well, I guess I can't just leave you standing on the doorstep like this, do come in," said Aunt Abigail.

"Um, Aunt Abigail, have you heard from my parents? Will they accept my return?" asked Elizabeth as she crossed the threshold of her Aunt's home. "Oh, don't worry about them, they'll come around. We're happy to have you home again. Don't listen to everything everyone says around here, you know how they are. Not everyone here agrees about anything, ever. You're not exactly new to these parts," said Aunt Abigail.

"Sorry to ask, but do you think there is a room I can nurse James?" asked Elizabeth. "It is his feeding time, and I don't want to make him wait too much longer." Elizabeth's Auntie led her down the hallway to her own bedroom, paused, opened the door just a crack, and said to her, "You know, I'm sorry we don't have enough space for you here but the community did do something for you that I think you'll like. You know who started the whole thing? That Wayne boy...he's a good boy, Elizabeth. You ought to thank him when you see him." "Oh, really," stated Elizabeth in a surprised manner. "I can't return to my parents' house?

she inquired. Not right now, Darlin', but don't you worry, everything will be okay."

After Elizabeth nursed James, Aunt Abigail recommended that they go and speak with Wayne and the owner of the small home where Elizabeth could stay. Her Aunt Abigail explained in a long-winded fashion the entire story about how nobody wanted to step up and help except Wayne, but one by one he had gained support from the majority of the community. When they arrived at the former shed which was now transformed into a miniature home, Elizabeth sighed relief and met the owner of the home. Thanking her profusely, she started to cry, thinking about where she came from and the road she had yet to cross. With tears of gratitude, she placed her bags down inside the home and gently placed James in a new crib which someone had built for her. Her tears were mixed with joy and sadness, but at least, she was home again.

The next day, Wayne came by the house to see if Elizabeth was settling into her home with James. "Good afternoon Miss Elizabeth, I see that you've made yourself at home. I just wanted to make sure you were alright since you're here alone with this cute little guy," said Wayne as he smiled at both Elizabeth and baby James. "Yes, thank you so much for everything you've done. Really, I could never have imagined that someone could do all of this for me, well, for us," replied Elizabeth. "Truly, you are an angel from heaven," continued Elizabeth.

"No, please, I'm just helping where I can," answered Wayne. "I can come back tomorrow and see if you're doing okay," he offered. "It's not necessary at all, but thank you very much," affirmed Elizabeth. "Can I get you anything to drink Wayne?" she asked. "If it's not too much trouble I would drink a glass of water," replied Wayne. "No trouble at all, really," said Elizabeth as she poured two glasses of water, one for each of them.

"So, how are you doing, Wayne? I haven't heard from you, of course, since before I left the community? Are you still helping with your family's farm? How is your mother? I always thought she was a lovely lady," acknowledged Elizabeth. "Thank you for asking, but I'm sorry to say that my mother passed away. She was always very ill when I was growing up," said Wayne. "Oh, I'm so terribly sorry. I didn't know. I feel awful," cried Elizabeth. "How could you have known? It's hard for me, but more so for my father. He's loved her since they were kids," acknowledged Wayne. "Now that it's just my father and me at the house there is also a lot of work to go around, but we manage alright," said Wayne. "I wish there was something I could do for you after all you have done for me," echoed Elizabeth.

"Just take care of yourself and your baby. I promise that I will come by the house when I can, even if you tell me not to. Only if you insist that I am not welcome, I will not come," said Wayne. "Well then, I guess, James and I wouldn't mind some company once in a while," she replied. "I apologize Ms. Elizabeth, but I have to meet my father for dinner. You won't mind if I leave, will you?" asked Wayne. "No, not at all," whispered Elizabeth, despite the fact that she was enjoying the company and a distraction from her heartache.

As Wayne excused himself and sauntered towards the door, Elizabeth followed him to the door to see him out, and Wayne extended his hand for a handshake, but Elizabeth decided a hug would be much more appropriate given the circumstance. Wayne's arms enclosed around Elizabeth like the wings of a dove, and she felt her spirit lifted by his warmth, his presence, and his support. Elizabeth found herself hugging him with an intensity that she did not expect, but she relished the embrace even after he had departed from her home. She found herself thinking about the hug from Wayne, but to the same extent she couldn't help but remember the feel of hugs from her husband. She was upset that she was starting to forget his smell. She had saved one of his favorite t-shirts, but his smell had long since disappeared from the shirt. Whilst the night folded around Elizabeth, baby James fell fast asleep in his new crib, and Elizabeth's eyed drooped and shut.

Chapter 7: From a Widow's Window

Despite Elizabeth's insistence that Wayne did not need to stop by the house on a daily basis, Wayne was true to his word, as a captain is to his crew during a storm at sea. Elizabeth had her own storm at sea, so to speak, and Wayne had slowly become her anchor. Elizabeth had never thought of Wayne in any other way than platonic before, but his frequent visits to the house gave her hope that James would have a semi-normal childhood. As she washed the dishes she caught herself looking out the window and watching Wayne hold little James. Her heart broke as she saw how good Wayne was with her baby, but she winced when she thought about how it should have been her husband holding James. She turned away quickly as she did not want the others to think additional bad things about her. As it was, the entire community seemed to be on edge with her decision to return to the community. Such a situation was completely unheard of, until her actually.

Even after turning away from the window she glanced again out the window at Wayne and James. Wayne reminded her oddly of her deceased husband, but only in a few ways. Elizabeth imagined that if her husband had been the chance to be a father to their baby he would have held little James the same way. Elizabeth couldn't seem to keep up with caring for James, herself, and the home, but Wayne was quite faithful in helping her. It seemed almost too nice. Who comes almost every day to care for a young widow, unless... thought Elizabeth... unless

Wayne had other interests. It finally occurred to her that Wayne maybe was interested in Elizabeth despite being a widow with a baby. Wayne saw her looking out the window at him. She waved innocently and quickly diverted her eyes back to her dishes, so she could pretend that she wasn't looking intentionally.

The problem was that Elizabeth felt torn emotionally in so many ways that she didn't know if she could be with someone else again ever. She didn't know if she should feel guilty for maybe even considering that she *MIGHT* like Wayne and that Wayne *MIGHT* like her. She felt *almost* like she did when she noticed that she had feelings for James after the first time they met. As guilt sunk in her smile turned upside down. Wayne re-entered the cottage shortly thereafter with baby James asleep in his arms. Although he could see something was wrong he didn't dare to ask what it was. He realized that they both were staring at each other through the window, but that probably was not a good topic of conversation.

"Well, can I help you with anything else? You sure look tired? I could watch James while you get some rest. He's asleep anyway. It's really no trouble at all Liz... Elizabeth. Sorry," stated Wayne. "You can call me Liz, it's not a problem. You don't have to be embarrassed. It's just, I'm amazed that you come here every day to help us. I'm certain that you have other people to care for, like yourself too, sometimes. Don't you think?" commented Elizabeth.

"Of course, but a good Amish man always respects an upstanding lady like yourself," replied Wayne. "If I didn't know any better, I'd think you were trying to charm me," said Elizabeth as she laughed and felt herself blush a little. "Well, maybe I am," Wayne said as he laughed a little before he continued, "I better be going then. I have to water the field. It's been hot these days and the crops just aren't growing like they should be." "Sure, good night then, and thank you, really," said Elizabeth. "Good night Liz," echoed Wayne as he walked away while a smile grew across his face.

Chapter 8: Baby Steps

The days passed for Wayne is a similar fashion. He worked the fields in the very early morning with his father. He prepared a light lunch for him and his father, took an afternoon siesta and then went to Liz's house around 3 pm every day, like clockwork. Wayne enjoyed his daily pattern but longed for something more with Liz. Although he didn't want to push her, especially considering that the two-year anniversary of her husband's death was approaching, he felt pulled towards her. Two years was more than one, but he knew very well that the heart healed only with time. Much as he felt with the passing of his own mother, he learned by day to grieve, but also to love, laugh, and smile again. Perhaps an even larger blessing than Liz or his father in his life was little baby James. Little baby James was not so little anymore and was growing into a healthy boy.

The first day that James took his first steps Wayne was at the house to watch him walk. While James walked to his mother, Elizabeth, who caught him and held him delicately in his arms, Wayne could not resist his own tears. Almost everything he could have dreamed of happening was already coming true. He didn't need to know everything, he didn't need to know the future with Liz and her son because in that moment everything was okay. In the face of everything they had passed together and separately, Elizabeth was coming to understand that everything he had done for her was not just out of respect, but also because he cared for her deeply.

Baby James turned with the help of his mother and started to take a few steps towards Wayne and uttered one syllable. Da. Wayne and Elizabeth could not have been happier or sadder as James grew and as they witnessed James walk and speak the word Da. In any case, Wayne was not James' biological father, but he was his father now, as much as his Elizabeth's husband was, if not more.

A few things were still missing from Elizabeth's life, including the acceptance of her parents and an understanding of what her relationship with Wayne was, but she stopped questioning it and accepted life as it was. She thought less about the English world, but she did occasionally receive visits from Meg, who wholeheartedly approved of Wayne, but did not yet utter it out loud. At least, in these moments, Elizabeth found peace, and her sense of self once more. She had an identity not just as a widow, but more importantly as a mother, a woman, and a friend. There were times, of course, that she still wondered what her life would be like if her husband had not passed away suddenly and unexpectedly, but she recognized that God was with her and would protect her always, and in a way, Wayne was the Holy Spirit, her dove, and little James, her son, symbolized Jesus Christ.

The stars were not always aligned in her favor, but a certain coffee-stained mug on her kitchen table was never empty to her. It was imperfect, but it was perfect to her. It was chipped on one side and the imperfectness of the mug was apparent to any stranger in her home, but to Elizabeth, the mug was like her home. The red lines across the center of the mug were slightly faded from use, and in her mind, the missing piece simply added character. Recently, a bright blue thumbprint had been added to the mug since James took a liking to paint. In spite of everything, life was whole, as whole as it could be, if you were a young Amish widow.

AMISH STRONG

130

MARISA MEYER

Chapter 1

Spring had awakened in the small Amish town, Mount Joy, birds were singing their spring interlude and blossoms covered the trees like frosting on a cake and the slight breeze carried its flowery sent through the village. But in the Fisher's home, it was the complete opposite. Rose Beiler's cousin Claire had gone into labour in the early hours of the morning and complications had set in. Somehow they had missed the fact she was pregnant with twins. One miracle baby had already been born and Rose was standing with the bundle in her arms while she looked on as the midwife tried her utmost to deliver the second one. Claire was in tremendous pain and agony and she had no more strength left to push.

"We need to get the Englisch doctor," Gretchen, the midwife said. Her voice desperate as she rubbed Claire's back where she lay on her side.

"And what would he do?" Rose's father muttered, standing with his straw hat in his hand.

Abraham Beiler had promised his sister on her death bed that he would protect Claire as if she was his own daughter, and with David, Claire's husband, having gone out of town, this was exactly what he was doing.

"The baby is not coming down, and it's in distress. He could do more than I can."

Rose watched her father tentatively. He was still very much old school, hated anything that represented the modern world and society. She could understand how he felt about cellular phones opening doors for evil to enter, but this was a matter of life and death. She adjusted the little baby's blanket and handed the child to the midwife.

"Daed, we cannot delay, if we don't call the Englisch doctor, Claire and the baby will die," she pleaded with her father. Her father studied her and a deep frown furrowed between his brows, the gentle touch of her hand on his arm brought his eyes to hers, "Please, we cannot lose Claire," she breathed.

"Fine!" he said frustrated, but his eyes were filled with concern.

Abraham was a muscular and tall man, people called him the Giant in jest because of his size, and although he may often come across as an intimidating individual, he had a soft heart. She knew that if he lost Claire because of his own stubbornness, he would never forgive himself, but sometimes he needed convincing.

Rose turned to her fiancé, Kemp, and nodded, "Go and hurry, Claire needs medical help urgently."

Kemp had been Rose's pillar of strength and from the age of sixteen it was a given that they would someday marry. It's been almost three years since he first made his intentions known and although their courtship had lasted a lot longer than most, she felt at ease and unburdened. She loved Kemp; he was a kind, generous and handsome man. Never had a harsh word to say and hardly ever got into any confrontations. Kemp also never said no whenever someone needed a helping hand. He was almost too good to be true.

Rose moved in next to her cousin and took her hand, "Hang in there, Kemp has gone to get the Englisch doctor, he will come and help."

Claire was incoherent and mumbled inaudibly, Rose sighed softly and said a silent prayer, then took a damp cloth to dab her cousin's feverish skin. Somewhere in the room the small cries of a newborn baby gave everyone a sparkle of hope. The midwife did everything possible to keep Claire comfortable while they waited for the doctor, but it felt as if time was in a suspended state.

An hour later, which felt like forever, Kemp burst into the kitchen and on his heels was the Englisch doctor, but it wasn't the doctor anyone expected.

"Where is Doctor Westbrook?" Abraham asked and looked out the door, half expecting him to come sauntering up the path.

"Good morning sir, I'm Dr Williams; unfortunately Dr Westbrook is at a conference in France..."

Abraham interrupted, "But you're so young."

Rose heard the commotion from the room and quickly got up to come and investigate and prevent Claire from getting too stressed.

She too was quite surprised when she got to the kitchen to find a strapping young man with a medical bag in his hand. Unlike Dr Westbrook who always arrived wearing his white coat, Dr Williams was dressed very casually, and she had to force herself to turn her attention back to the pressing matter.

"Daed, just let the doctor get on with it," Claire said and stood aside.

Dr Williams smiled confidently, "I can assure you Mr Beiler, I'm more than capable of assisting. Kemp mentioned that Claire is in labour?"

"Yah-yah, she is," Said Claire, wringing her hands nervously, "We did not know she was expecting twins. The midwife is with her, but she is not knowledgeable enough to help her."

Dr Williams nodded and skirted past Rose's father and nodded courteously at her. She glanced back at Kemp and Abraham. The concern etched on their faces matched hers. Two years ago they had buried her aunt, Claire's mother after she passed away due to pneumonia, and she knew that her father could not cope with another death in the family. *Be positive Rose*, she told herself before disappearing into the room and closing the door behind her. The less her father got to see, the better and until Claire was out of danger and the second infant was born, she would stay by her cousin's side. She just wishes David was here to support his wife.

David and Claire got married last fall, and although they looked like a happy couple on the outside, everything wasn't as peachy behind closed doors. When they first met, it wasn't a case of falling in love, it was an arranged betrothal, one Rose was opposed against, but everyone insisted that Claire marry before she turned thirty. Her mother had been overly concerned that she would end up becoming a spinster. When the bow finally broke and Claire agreed, she was introduced to David. He was from a neighbouring Amish community, only two days away by carriage. A few months after their marriage however, David kept making excuses to go back home, where he would stay for days at a time. No one else knew this, but Claire had told her that she suspected that David had another flame burning elsewhere, but it was not her place to make such accusations. Especially since David was the Bishop's son, so instead, Claire decided to simply turn a blind eye and hope it will all blow over one day.

Rose was convinced that all the stress and anxiety Claire had to deal with was the cause for her current predicament, and deep down she hated David for being so selfish. In the last few hours she had to repent more than once for feeling so angry towards him. Naturally, knowing how hard it had been for Claire to cope, she couldn't help but be nervous about her own engagement to Kemp. Especially since Kemp and David were friends. There was always that nagging voice in the back of her mind, asking her if he was really the right man for her and if she too, would one day become a lifeless bag of bones, living each day with no purpose.

No! She couldn't entertain these negative thoughts, Kemp was nothing like David she scolded herself and shook her head. Right now there were more important things at stake.

"When was the other baby born?" the doctor asked.

"About two hours ago," she said nervously.

"Did she have any difficulties with the birth?"

"I don't know Doctor, she gave birth, and it's not the easiest thing to do as is. What is wrong with her?"

He looked up at her and hooked his stethoscope in his ears and placed the end piece on Claire's abdomen; he listened tentatively and moved it around slowly. She couldn't help but notice the colour of his eyes. He had two different colour eyes, one hazel and one with a slight tinge of blue, which she found rather unusual. Again she had to remind herself to focus.

"Without a Caesarean section, the baby will not make it," he said and came around to look under the blanket.

"Is it that serious?" Rose asked, biting her lip.

"I'm afraid so, she's unconscious and in no position to give natural birth right now."

"Is she going to have to go to hospital?" Claire asked worriedly.

"There's no time," he said and moved around to his medical bag, "We will have to do it here."

"What!?" she cried out.

Rose's stomach bottomed out and her hand flew to her mouth, but his words were barely cold when her father stormed into the room demanding to know what was going on.

Rose calmed him down and get Kemp to take him outside while she stayed behind to assist. Everything had happened so fast, and a few minutes later, Claire's second baby was born healthy.

Chapter 2

Grant had known that Dr Westbrook had a special group of patients he did house calls to occasionally but what he didn't expect was for them to be Amish. When the guy on the carriage pulled up in front of the medical practice, he was rather intrigued, until he discovered why he had come.

What he knew of the Amish was what he had seen on TV and online, so when he arrived there he had no idea what he was in for. But he was pleasantly surprised. Other than Mr Beiler who was a little sceptic the others were rather pleasant. Kemp was a quiet individual, he only said what was needed and didn't bother to hold much conversation. The mid-wife clearly knew what she was doing; otherwise the other baby would have gone through the same trouble. And as for the girl, whose name he learned was Rose, she was a lot more verbal than the rest. She looked like the type who could take charge if the walls came tumbling down and throughout the procedure, she remained calm and collected, following his instructions to the T.

Both babies were healthy enough, not in need of medical attention. But Claire would need a few weeks to recover, which meant he would have make daily trips to Mount Joy to check on her. At least next time around he would drive here in his own car, which would probably take 10 minutes instead of an hour.

"Dr Williams," Rose said as he headed to the door.

"Yes Rose?"

"I just wanted to thank you for saving Claire and the baby today."

"You can call me Grant," he said and smiled, "It's what I'm there for."

"I know, but thank you anyway... Grant," she smiled appreciatively.

He nodded just as Kemp pushed past him to go outside so he stepped out of the man's way, and reached out to touch Rose's shoulder, "I'll be back tomorrow to check on them."

Rose flinched, and he immediately knew he had overstepped some sort of boundary. He really needed to brush up on Amish culture and understand the do's and do not's.

Chapter 2

The next day arrived with much promise and anticipation, Grant convinced himself that it was the mystery of this small Amish village that attracted him. It had nothing to do with the blue eyed woman in the plain purple dress and white apron, whose blonde hair was neatly tucked under her bonnet. For a moment while they worked to save the baby and Claire, he had wondered what she would look like with her hair loose.

As he drove into the small town, he was surprised to see far less people around than first expected. Compared to the day before, the town was almost half deserted and it was already past ten in the morning. Surely they would all be up and busy doing what Amish people do, by now. He pulled to a stop in front of the Beiler home and got out of his car. Even the house was quiet, and the curtains were still drawn. He contemplated waiting but as he turned to get back into his car, the front door opened.

"Dr Williams, I'm so sorry, I was busy helping Claire feed the babies."

His heart rate increased a fraction at the site of her and her half smile that caused the dimples in her cheeks to appear like wishing wells.

"Is it a convenient time or should I come back," he said. He had to remain professional. He was a doctor or heaven's sake.

"It's perfectly fine," said Rose and opened the door wider, "She's been resting, but the babies have been very restless."

Grant did whatever necessary to keep his mind focused on Claire and the babies, but with Rose hovering around like a mother hen protecting her chicks, he found it extra trying to concentrate.

"So how are you feeling Claire?" he asked, diverting his attention fully to his patient.

Claire flinched as she pushed herself up a little, "I'm fine, I'm so sorry you had to go through all the trouble to come out here."

"Oh don't apologize, it's what I do for a living, I'm just glad we saved both you and the baby. So have you named them yet?"

Claire shook her head and lowered her eyes, "No, I have to wait for my husband to return."

Rose snorted behind him, "David doesn't deserve you Claire."

"Rose! Don't talk like that." Claire looked at him, "David is a busy man, he will be here by the end of the week."

Grant noted immediately that Rose clearly did not like this David fellow, but again, it was not his place. He did however feel sorry for Claire having to have gone through this all on her own.

"And you Rose?" he asked casually not wanting to sound too fishy.

"What about me?"

"Do you have any children or a husband?"

There was a moment of silence and he looked up at her. She stood with her lips pursed and a slight frown etched on her forehead. Did he overstep again? He wondered.

"She's not married," Claire piped up.

"Claire!" Rosa reprimanded.

"What, it's the truth, you and Kemp have been courting, but nothing ever comes of it," Claire muttered and then reached to touch Grant's hand, "I think she's too afraid."

"What utter nonsense! I'm not afraid; I just don't see why I should rush anything."

Grant chuckled but didn't interject.

"What about you Doctor, are you married?"

"Oh for heaven's sake Clair, do you have to be so quizzical!" Rose reprimanded.

Grant smiled and shook his head, "I was married, but my wife is no longer alive, it's been almost four years."

"Oh goodness, I'm so sorry for your loss," Claire said with genuine sympathy.

Rose bit her lip and held her hand over her chest. The poor man must still grieve the loss of his wife and Claire is non-the-wiser.

Chapter 3

Rose was shocked that Claire would announce her status so carelessly, and of all things holy, what gave Dr Williams the right to ask such personal questions. She had stormed out of the room and stood waiting in the living room for him to finish what he came to do while pacing impatiently. What was it about this man? Since the day he walked into this house, there was this strange feeling of longing that suddenly rose up within her soul. It was as if she was missing something in her life, but she couldn't quite put her finger on it. Maybe it was seeing Claire in such peril that made her realize just how short life was, or maybe it was the miracle of birth. She was already nearing thirty and soon her father would pressurise her into marriage, and she was still not sure if it was what she wanted, and the arrival of the Englisch doctor didn't help her either.

She was just a little girl when she had found a little fox trapped in one of the fences that bordered Mount Joy. Her first instinct was to free the poor animal, which she did and since then she always wanted to help animals. She had discovered much later, that in order to be a Veterinarian, she would need to study, but that was against God's will. Or so her father said. *A woman's place is in the kitchen, caring for her husband and children,* her father had said countless times. But while she was still unmarried, she had the freedom to tend to the horses when the men were not around. A lot of the girls laughed at her and told her she was foolish, but she never let that get her down.

She twisted the string of her bonnet around her finger as she glanced out of the window and sighed. What if she was being foolish? Maybe it was time for her to settle down and start a family of her own.

"Rose?"

Grant's voice broke into her train of thought and she turned around.

"Claire is doing as well as expected, but I will have to come back again to make sure the incision does not become septic."

Rose nodded and walked to the door, her heart racing for no reason, "I will keep an eye on her too."

Grant walked to the door but before he exited the house, he stopped and faced her, "I didn't mean to pry into your life," he whispered.

She wanted to respond to that, but her brain and her lips were suddenly disconnected. She opened her mouth to speak but nothing came out. And then unexpectedly, Grant leaned forward and pressed his lips against hers. Rose froze instantly, her arms like steel against her sides but her insides were wreaking havoc. Her heart fluttered wildly in her chest and her stomach had filled with a kaleidoscope of butterflies, all flapping their colourful wings at once.

When Grant raised his head, and the moment had passed, she slowly opened her eyes and looked into his deep soulful eyes.

"I-I'm sorry, I shouldn't have done that," he said immediately. He raised his hand as if to touch her cheek but withdrew it as if the contact would burn his fingers.

Realization swept over Rose followed by an immense feeling of guilt. She had just allowed an Englisch man to kiss her, and that while she was promised to another. Without a word she almost shoved him out the door and slammed the door shut. How could she have allowed herself to be so foolish! She had committed an adulterous sin and for that she knew she was going to be punished. But even then she could still feel the warmth of his lips on hers, and it felt so right, and so natural.

The sound of his car drifted further and further away, and only once she could no longer hear it, did she peek out of the window. Thankfully there were very few people in town this morning since they had all gone to a barn raising. She was horrified at the thought of what would happen had anyone witnessed what had just happened. She brought her trembling fingers to her lips and she let out a sigh.

"Rose!" Claire called from the room.

Rose took a deep steadying breath, fixed her bonnet and raised her chin. No one needed to know what happened, and when the doctor comes again, she would make sure she was not around. After all, she never returned the kiss.

"Do you need anything?" she asked her cousin.

"Dr Williams is a great man," she said and Rose swallowed.

"He is handy to have around," she mumbled.

"He likes you."

Rose's eyes grew as wide as saucers and she regarded her cousin, "He's Englisch, just because he asked me about my status, doesn't mean he likes me," she muttered.

"I saw the way he looked at you."

"He probably looks at every woman like that."

"Not the way he looked at you, he was taken by you."

Rose threw her hands up and shook her head, "Why are we having this conversation? Even if he liked me, you know very well that it's futile, he's not Amish. Besides, I'm happily engaged to a wonderful man, thank you very much."

Claire reached for Rose's hand and squeezed it, "Don't make the same mistakes I made, just look where that has gotten me."

Rose bent down and brushed a stray strand of hair from her cousin's face, "It's gotten you two beautiful children, and maybe, just maybe by God's grace, this is the exact thing David needs to realize what an amazing wife he has."

Claire's eyes shot full of tears and she shook her head, "No, that will never change. Maybe if we had met without the intervention of the bishop and we let things advance naturally, there would have been hope, but David does not love me. He tolerates the notion of marriage and respects the faith."

"Oh Claire," Rose said and carefully hugged her cousin, "God works in mysterious ways, he would not have put you two together was it not His will."

Claire didn't reply, simply sniffed and then plastered a brave smile on her face, "At least you and Kemp got to know each other."

"Exactly, so I'm very happy with my engagement and there's no reason for my eyes to wander to a certain doctor simply because he's handsome."

Claire laughed wholeheartedly, "So you do think he's handsome!"

"There's no denying that!"

The two women spent the rest of the morning talking about life, Rose helped Claire to feed the twins and she bathed and dressed them and saw to nappy changes. It kept her mind busy to say the least, and for the time being she forced herself not to pay a single thought of Dr Williams.

Chapter 4

It was a lovely spring morning, and like every other morning so far, Grant was getting ready to head out to Mount Joy to see to his patient. He was about to leave when his receptionist announced that he had a visitor.

"Send him in," he said and put down the receiver.

It was Kemp who entered the rooms and although Grant was poised and calm, his insides were in a knot.

"Kemp, what brings you to town?" he asked casually.

Kemp took his hat off and clutched it in front of him, "Dr Williams, I'm sorry to barge in like this, but I was wondering if I may have a word with you?"

Uh-oh, Grant thought as he gestured for Kemp to take a seat. First thing that crossed his mind was the kiss, what if Kemp had seen it?

"So what can I do for you?" he asked curiously.

Kemp cleared his throat and sat down, "You know about the Amish yah?"

Grant nodded not sure where this was going, "A little, but not much, why?"

"Well, in the Amish, men may not study, if they do, they have to leave the community, which means they will be shunned."

Confused, Grant leaned forward on his elbows and regarded the man in front of him, "So if you want to further your education you are not allowed to?"

He nodded his head and looked down, "The thing is, I want to do what you do, I want to be a doctor and as long as I am at Mount Joy, I can't realize my dream."

Grant studied the man and he could understand exactly how conflicted he must be, "So if you decide to study, you cannot go back to Mount Joy?"

Kemp shook his head, "Yah, I can go back, but I will be like you, Englisch, I won't be able to partake in certain things, and I won't be able to marry Rose. But you see, Rose and I..."

The rest of the conversation was muted by Grant's own thoughts at realizing that Kemp was Rose' fiancé and just yesterday, he had so boldly overstepped his welcome by kissing her.

"... she will understand," Kemp said and sat back.

Grant hadn't heard a single word he was saying and shifted awkwardly in his chair.

"How do you think she would feel?" he shot in the dark.

"Rose is a strong woman, I care for her greatly but she will not stand in my way if I wish to become a doctor."

This was just too overwhelming, he thought. If Kemp was considering leaving behind everything he knew that meant he would leave Rose behind too. There was a flutter of excitement in his insides and he sat steeping his fingers together.

"I think you need to speak to Rose and tell her exactly how you feel."

Kemp nodded and then stood up, "That is what I intend to do."

Later that same day, Grant had visited Claire, but Rose was nowhere to be seen. Worried that Kemp may have spoken to her, to tell her about his plans and how she would take it, he had very nonchalantly asked Clair where she was. She was also not sure where her cousin was, but told him to wait around if he wanted to see her. He didn't, it was far too awkward, not knowing head or tail how Rose felt. He too, had some conflict, after his wife Angelique died of leukaemia he vowed never to marry again. He had loved his wife almost more than life itself and what was the hardest part of all was the fact that despite his qualifications as a medical doctor, he could do nothing about the disease that claimed his wife's life. So naturally, these feelings that started out of nowhere for a woman he hardly knew was just as much a surprise as the fact that he was falling for an Amish woman.

Over the next week or two, Grant made regular trips to the town and slowly got to know more and more of the community, occasionally he saw Rose, and although he yearned to talk to her, he couldn't bring himself to do so. She was like that breath of fresh air, a city boy needed, to get a new lease on life, but she was indefinitely out of his reach.

Kemp was also still around, and it didn't look like he had made any effort to talk to Rose about his feelings towards studying further, which led him to believe that Kemp was going to simply stay put and submit to the laws of his kin.

Chapter 5

A month had passed, and Grant was still a regular visitor to Mount Joy, the resident doctor, the community dubbed him. But every day it had become harder and harder for Rose to cope. Her father was pressing her to decide and marry Kemp. But every time she laid eyes on Grant, she knew beyond the shadow of a doubt that she couldn't marry Kemp, not while her heart was torn in two.

It was one morning when she went to collect eggs from the chicken coop that she stole some time for herself. She needed God to guide her and help her make the right choices. She needed Him to rid her of these feelings of desire and guilt. She placed the egg basket on one of the crates and knelt down.

"Almighty God and Heavenly Father, you who know everyone's heart and failings, and who know the secrets we keep hidden, I ask you to help and comfort, and I beg you for guidance during this time. Forgive me my sins, which I have committed against you in word or deed, knowingly or unknowingly. I pray this in Your Holy name. Amen."

She had just gotten up off her knees when she heard a noise outside the coop and she went to investigate, it was Kemp and David, who had eventually returned to help Claire with the children. Afraid that they would notice her, she stayed hidden behind the wooden wall.

"I want to leave this place," she heard Kemp say.

"And go where?" asked David.

"I spoke to the Englisch doctor, I told him that I wanted to study further and also become a doctor."

Rose couldn't believe her ears, with her hand cupped over her mouth to quieten her breaths; she listened tentatively as Kemp told David that he was not ready to settle down. David warned him of the consequences of his actions too, but Kemp already had his heart set on leaving the Amish community, not so much the faith, but just to explore the world and find a bigger purpose.

Her heart ached in her chest, because like him, she always wanted to be a woman of purpose, not a simple girl working in the kitchen and seeing to a man's every need. Perhaps, this was the sign God had sent her, she thought quietly and waited for the two men to leave again. But even if this was a sign that she was not to be married now, what good would that do? She could still not consider the Englisch doctor, it was and absurd notion to say the least, and her father would have a cadenza. She was undoubtedly still stuck between a rock and a hard place, but at least it was a step closer to freedom. As soon as the two men left, she hurried to collect all the eggs, but as she stepped out of the chicken coop, the very object of her desire came walking across the field towards her. She stopped in her tracks, and even considered throwing the eggs at him to keep him away from her, but that would be silly.

"Rose, Claire told me I could find you here," he called with that heart stopping smile tugging at the corners of his lips.

"I was collecting eggs, is Claire all right?" she asked curiously.

"She's fine," he said as he stopped in front of her, "I wanted to apologise to you."

"What for?" *Apologise for the kiss or for falling into my life so unexpectedly, or for causing me to doubt my place in the Amish faith?* Her thoughts rallied.

"The kiss, I was completely out of line, and I wanted to apologise for my behaviour," he said as he crossed his arms over his chest, "I swear to you that I haven't told a single soul and I would never disgrace you."

She was surprised by his actions, but more so, she questioned them. Was he apologizing because he no longer desired her, or because he came to his senses and realized that there could be nothing between them?

"I forgive you," she simply said and gathered her skirt before sweeping past him like a gentle breeze.

"Rose..." he said, and she stopped.

"I-I don't regret it, and if I had another chance, I would do it again. You are a beautiful woman."

She felt her cheeks heat up, and she lowered her gaze, avoiding eye contact was the only thing that would keep her from dropping the eggs and running into his arms to just have one more kiss. She didn't respond to his admission though, instead, she turned and headed back towards the house, but all the while she could feel his eyes on her.

At dinner, Rose, Claire, David and Abraham sat quietly at the table; there was an eerie silence in the room.

"Is everything okay uncle?" Claire asked curiously.

"All is well," Abraham said as he poked around his plate.

Claire gave a shrug and continued eating, but Rose couldn't ignore the dreadful feeling of hopelessness that filled her insides.

"Kemp is leaving Mount Joy," Abraham said after a while, and both Claire and Rose gasped, and although Rose already knew, the finality of it came as a shock.

"He's leaving?" Claire uttered.

"Yah," David said, "He wants to study further."

Her father nodded and reached for Rose's hand, "You will find another suitor my child, if this is God's will then so be it, do not let it trouble you."

"But why didn't he tell me in person?" she asked, feigning disappointment.

"He couldn't bear hurting you, he left earlier today, but he told me to tell you that he'll always care for you," said David and dug into the potatoes.

"But we were going to marry!" Rose objected, placing her knife and fork down on the table.

"Only if God willed it," Abraham said and then continued with his meal, "The Lord, clearly has other plans for you."

Rose glanced towards Claire whose mouth was still gaping, and instead of being heartbroken she smiled at Claire, who raised an amused brow.

"I suppose it's for the best then," Claire breathed and reached for Rose's hand, "You'll find a wonderful husband yet."

Rose smiled and thanked God silently for hearing a part of her prayer at least. It had brought another season of freedom, which meant she could come and go as she pleased without the noose of marriage; to a man she cared for but didn't truly love, hanging around her neck.

As Claire got up to clear the dishes, Abraham cleared his throat, "Oh and another thing, the Englisch doctor decided to embrace the

Amish faith, and the Bishop agreed that he can continue his practice here and serve the community."

Claire dropped a plate, and it shattered on the floor and Rose nearly leaped off of her chair with excitement, but she stayed calm and collected.

"Well that's just brilliant! We could use the skill of a qualified doctor around here," Claire exclaimed as she started cleaning up her mess.

Abraham nodded, "Indeed, after what you had to endure, it didn't take much to convince the elders."

"Isn't that wonderful Rose?" Claire exclaimed but Rose simply nodded and smiled awkwardly.

In the back of the house, the wail of the twins echoed and David and Claire rushed to attend to the hungry infants.

Chapter 6

Grant stood on the porch outside of his new home in Mount Joy; he had made a brave move to adopt the Amish faith. Not only because he secretly hoped to win the hand of Rose Beiler, but because something deep down evoked a feeling a desire to have a more substantial connection with God. The realisation that he had lost his faith came as unexpectedly as his growing feelings for Rose. All his life he had worked towards saving lives, treating illnesses and being the prophet of doom for telling families that their loved ones had passed away. And when his wife died, he somehow blamed God. It was at that time that he realized just how insignificant life really was. In the end all the knowledge he had gained and practiced could save some lives, but it could never save souls. Raised in a Christian home, he had the foundation of faith, but never really lived it. But ever since visiting this community, and as days turned into weeks and he got to spend more time with these people, he started to slowly realise that he needed to choose for the sake of his soul.

His first day as an Amish community member, had come to an end and although he was yet to be baptised, the folk were treating him like one of their own and he couldn't have asked for anything better. He was about to turn in for the evening when Rose came walking up the small path to his house and his heart thrummed in his chest.

"Good evening Rose," he said and smiled.

"Evening to you Grant, I just came to bring you some dinner. It was Claire's idea."

Grant chuckled and took the dish from Rose, "Well, your cousin clearly knows when a man needs to be fed."

Rose laughed softly and tucked a strand of hair behind her ear, "Indeed she does, anyway, may the Lord bless you."

She turned to leave, but Grant stopped her, "Do you want to have dinner with me?" he asked.

Rose laughed and shook her head, "I don't think that would be appropriate," she said but then turned and looked at him, "Maybe once you're baptised, you can offer me a ride in your buggy to a sing gathering, or to one of the church services."

Grant studied her and smirked, "Are you playing hard to get?"

"I'm playing by the rules," she said and smiled.

Grant held back the urge to pull her into his arms and silently thanked God that he had a dish in his hands, "I think I need to get my hands on the rule book and familiarise myself with these customs."

Rose laughed and swept down and plucked a small Daisy from the flower pot on the porch, "That would be wise notion doctor," she whispered and smiled before laying the daisy on top of the dish he held in his hands.

"Wise indeed, so do you promise to let me take you to the church service once I have been baptised?" he asked teasingly.

"Only if you promise to behave," she joked.

"I swear on my life," he chuckled.

~*~

A few months later, Rose stood outside the house, with Claire peeking through the window ever two minutes. Her heart was beating out of control as she waited for Grant to arrive. He had finally been baptised and although it was almost impossible to stay away from him, she managed to do so by the grace of God and hours of praying and fasting.

When Grant finally arrived, and he got out of the buggy, he grinned and walked up the stairs to meet her.

"It's been a trying time for me," he whispered as he looked down at her.

"But worth the wait?" she teased.

Grant smiled and moved his hand from behind his back holding a single Daisy in his hand, "Would you do me the honour of allowing me to take you to church?"

From inside the house, Rose could hear Claire squeal with delight and she couldn't help but laugh.

"I would be delighted," she whispered and gently took the daisy from him and placed it in her bible.

Genesis 2:18 The LORD God said, "It is not good for the man to be alone. I will make a helper suitable for him."

AMISH DEPARTURE

DEIDRA SCOTT

Chapter One

Lizzy Swartz closed her eyes and took in a deep breath of the spring air. The scent of cut grass and freshly plowed dirt put a smile on her face. She lifted her face upward, allowing the sun to warm her skin.

There was nothing like a spring day spent working out in the garden. Just the time in God's outdoors put a song in Lizzy's heart.

Suddenly, something hard hit her in the arm. Lizzy opened her eyes to see her fifteen-year-old brother, Abe, preparing to launch another clod of dirt in her direction.

"*Ach*, Abe!" Lizzy exclaimed, "Will ya never start to grow up?"

Abe stood up straighter and gave his dirt ball a toss across the garden, "Probably not," he replied, a boyish grin spreading across his handsome face.

Lizzy couldn't help but smile back, "Well, don't just stand there – pick up a garden hoe and get to work!"

"Yes, ma'am!" Abe returned in a silly tone and anxiously grabbed one of the tools, "I wouldn't want you to decide to whack me *gut* with one."

"Where's Grandpa?" Lizzy asked as she set to work chopping out some of the weeds that were starting to grow between the rows.

"He ran out to the mailbox," Abe replied.

They worked in silence for a few minutes until Abe finally asked, "Lizzy, what do you think would have happened to us if Grandpa hadn't taken us in?"

Abe's question made Lizzy stop for a moment. My, but hadn't she asked herself that question at least a dozen times? It had been almost twelve years since their parents had been killed in a tragic buggy wreck. The Amish community had been hit by hard times already with a rough drought that killed most of the area crops and left everyone feeling the strain financially. No one had enough money to take on two extra Amish children. At one point, there had been talk of sending Lizzy and Abe to foster care...but then Grandpa had stepped in.

A widower who was already shouldering the heavy job of being bishop to the Amish community, Grandpa had taken them in as if they were his own children. Although they called him Grandpa, he was completely unrelated to Lizzy and Abe.

"I don't know, Abe," Lizzy finally said with a deep sigh, "But I certainly thank God every day for sending him our way."

Abe slowly nodded his head, "*Jah*, me too."

They both worked in silence.

Grandpa had not provided them with a fancy life full of impressive possessions, but he had done his part to give them a stable home that was rich in love. Over the years, he had worked hard to instill steady morals, a love for their Creator, and a respect for hard work in the hearts of both Lizzy and her brother.

"Have you got any plans for tonight?" Abe finally asked.

Lizzy felt her face go red with embarrassment. "*Ach*, Abe," she exclaimed, "Aren't you a nosey one! Maybe I do and maybe I don't!"

"I already know you're going out with Matt Christner!" Abe exclaimed, tossing another clod of dirt at his sister, "I saw him in town and he told me."

"Well, isn't he the big mouth!" Lizzy returned with a laugh.

While Lizzy and Matt had been friends for most of their lives, they had only recently started dating. Although their relationship was new, Lizzy had already recognized that Matt was the man she wanted to eventually marry.

Lizzy's thoughts were cut short when she heard Grandpa whistling as he walked up behind her.

"Mail's here!" He announced cheerfully as he handed Lizzy a letter from her cousin in Pennsylvania.

"Didn't I get anything?" Abe asked.

"You can open mine," Grandpa told him with a laugh, tossing a handful of envelopes in his direction, "Let me know if I got anything other than bills. I'm going out to the calf barn to check on some of the babies."

Abe flipped the mail around in his hand, sorting through it for anything exciting. Stopping at one envelope, he gave a shrug and tore it open.

"Oh, Abe," Lizzy let out a laugh as she started to read the letter from her cousin, "Sally says..."

"Wait, Lizzy!" Abe exclaimed, cutting her short. Before she could protest, he called out, "Grandpa, come back here! It's important!"

Grandpa turned and hurried back to Abe's side, anxious to see what was wrong.

"*Ach*, what's happened now?" He asked, reaching for the letter.

"It nothing bad, Grandpa!" Abe exclaimed, "Its good news! Your uncle who died left you a lot of money! A lot! Yee-haw!"

"Well, I'll be," Grandpa whispered as he scanned over the document, "It surely does look like I've inherited quite a sum of money...from an uncle I don't even remember."

As Grandpa read the letter once more, Abe gave his hat a toss in the air and grabbed his sister by the shoulders, "Lizzy...we're rich!"

Chapter Two

Until Grandpa had a chance to go see the lawyer in town, they all three agreed not to tell a soul about the letter or the possibility of the inheritance. While Abe was convinced that they truly were now wealthy, neither Lizzy nor Grandpa shared his confidence.

That night, Lizzy's boyfriend Matt arrived at their house on his buggy. Although it was hard to think of anything other than the inheritance, getting to go somewhere with Matt seemed like it might distract her from the thought of money.

As she rode along beside Matt on his buggy, Lizzy found that the idea of getting her mind on something else was entirely too far-fetched to be possible.

Suddenly, Lizzy realized that Matt had hardly spoken a word to her since he picked her up at her house.

"*Ach*, Matt," she muttered, suddenly feeling ashamed of herself, "Here we've been riding together for miles and I've hardly spoken a word this whole trip. I'm sorry. I'd better watch it or you'll be picking you out a new sweetheart!"

Turning to look at Matt, she realized that he wasn't laughing or even smiling at her comments. Instead, it seemed like a dark cloud was over his handsome face.

"You shouldn't be apologizing, Lizzy," Matt replied with a deep sigh as he turned the reigns over in his hands, "I should be the one doing that. I'm not much company tonight. Probably not the best day to be takin' ya out to eat, but I sure hated to cancel. Wouldn't want you to pick out a new beau either."

Studying her boyfriend's sad face made Lizzy feel like crying herself. She knew that her Matt had been going through a rough year. His mom had been diagnosed with cancer and, although the treatments seemed to be working, Lizzy realized the family was still dealing with a lot of stress and uncertainty.

Reaching out to pat him on the shoulder, Lizzy found herself searching for the right words to say but coming up short.

"Matt," she finally said with a sigh, "The Lord hasn't forgotten about your family – he has a plan."

Matt slowly nodded his head, but Lizzy wondered if his faith was getting shaky.

The next morning, Grandpa got up early to hitch up the buggy and drive into town to see a lawyer. Although Grandpa warned Lizzy and Abe that the letter was probably nothing more than just a fake, it was impossible not to notice the hopeful glimmer in his eyes.

Waiting for Grandpa to get home was about enough to drive Lizzy mad. The hours seemed to pass so slowly and, every time Lizzy glanced toward the driveway, her heart sank as she realized Grandpa was no where in sight.

Trying to make the time pass faster, Lizzy busied herself with chores around the house. By afternoon, Lizzy had already scrubbed all of the hardwood floors, hosed off the porch, and washed the windows.

"Still no sign of Grandpa?" Abe asked as he stepped into the kitchen, looking for an afternoon snack.

Lizzy shook her head as she lowered one of the windows, "I hope he's okay."

The barking of their dog sent both Lizzy and Abe to the front door.

"He's home!" Abe squealed, jumping like a little kid as he pushed past Lizzy and started out toward the barn where Grandpa was unhitching the horses.

Not wanting to be left out, Lizzy followed close behind her brother.

By the time they reached the barn, both Lizzy and Abe were out of breath.

"Grandpa," Abe gasped, grabbing his side with his hand, "Grandpa, what happened? What did he say?"

"Help me unhitch the horses, Abe," Grandpa replied solemnly as his leathery hands set to work taking the bits out of the animals' mouths.

Abe stepped up and started working alongside his grandfather, his mouth still going much faster than his fingers, "But Grandpa, what happened in town?"

"*Ach*, Abe, we'll talk once we're all inside."

"But we're all out here, Grandpa!"

Despite Abe's pleading, Grandpa remained firm. Watching him lead the horses to an empty stall where he poured them some fresh oats, Lizzy felt her heart sink. There was no way the letter could have been true.

Once they were finished, Grandpa sat down at the kitchen table while Lizzy hurried to set a plate of fresh cookies and a glass of milk in front of him.

"Sit down, Lizzy. Sit down, Abe." Grandpa instructed.

Abe practically jumped into his seat and Lizzy felt like she couldn't grab the chair fast enough.

"Children," Grandpa finally said with a laugh, "I don't know how to tell you this...but the letter was real and the money is now in the bank. We truly are rich!"

Chapter Three

While Grandpa wouldn't say just how much money he had inherited, Lizzy realized that it must be a lot.

Sitting around the table that night, Grandpa explained that the money was something they needed to use for good purposes.

"I know how easy it is to simply waste money," Grandpa told them as he finished off Lizzy's delicious meal of homemade sweet rolls, applesauce, fried potatoes, and pork chops, "And I don't want us to waste what we have now. Before we start spending a lot of it, I want you two to come up with some ways that we could use the money to do something *gut*...not just for ourselves, but for the entire community."

Abe lowered his head, obviously a bit disappointed at the thought of having to share with the rest of the Amish.

"Can we buy a few things for ourselves?" Abe asked with 'humph'.

"Of course," Grandpa opened up his wallet and began sorting through his bills, "I know that there are things around the house that we need. Lizzy," he motioned for her to hold out her hand, "This is for you and Abe to spend on the things that we need."

Unfolding the bills that Grandpa had placed in her hand, Lizzy gasped as she whispered, "*Ach*, Grandpa, this is one-thousand dollars!"

Grandpa nodded slowly, "I think it's time that we made some improvements around here. Let me know if you need more than that."

Staring at the money, Lizzy wondered how on earth she could ever begin to think of spending one-thousand dollars on anything.

The next morning, Lizzy discovered that spending money was much easier than she had expected. When she had her driver take her to the grocery store, she planned to only spend within her usual budget. For the last five years, Grandpa had given Lizzy the sole responsibility of shopping for their weekly groceries with a very small amount of money. Lizzy had learned how to be resourceful by making purchases in bulk, off-brand items, and using coupons.

As she entered the store that Thursday morning, it seemed harder than ever to stick to her budget. Just knowing that she had one-thousand dollars to use as she saw fit made shopping seem like an entirely different experience.

When she left the grocery, Lizzy had a cart load full of groceries she would never normally purchase. After seeing how high the bils was, Lizzy promised herself she would start using their money more wisely.

Despite Lizzy's resolution to be more careful with the money, it seemed less possible with each day that passed.

Grandpa and Abe were astonished with her expensive meals that included thick steaks, but enjoyed them so much that she wasn't scolded; in fact, Grandpa reminded her to keep buying what they needed because the money was unlimited.

Although Lizzy had always enjoyed baking, the convenience of running to the store to pick up ready-to-eat loaves of bread, pies, and cookies was almost more than she could stand.

When wash day came, Lizzy even hired a driver to take her to the local laundry mat where she was able to get them cleaned and dried in a fraction of the time it took her to do the job by hand at home.

As soon as Lizzy realized that some of their clothing needed to be patched, she chose to toss the damaged items in the trash rather than keep them. When she went to pick out new fabric, the thought of sewing sounded so time consuming, that she simply hired one of the local Amish seamstresses to do the work for her.

While her work load dwindled, Lizzy took the opportunity to enjoy time reading books and going on walks in the fields.

Lizzy wasn't the only one who enjoyed the chance to indulge in some expensive luxuries. Grandpa decided that, rather than clean out the barn by hand, he would hire someone with a bobcat to do it for him.

"We need to make some serious barn repairs, too." Grandpa told Abe and Lizzy, "I'm thinking we could just hire a team of the Amish carpenters to come fix it up for us." Pausing for a moment to think, he added, "Honestly, might be even more sensible to just build a new barn all together."

"Grandpa," Luke started slowly, "I'll be sixteen next month and the age to go to the young peoples' gatherings. Do ya suppose you could just buy me a new buggy to drive? The old one's so worn out and it sure sends me in the air when I hit a bump – I'd hate to find me a pretty girl and send her sailing off the buggy seat!"

They all laughed and Grandpa nodded, "*Jah*, I don't see how a new buggy could hurt!"

Within a few days, the entire family wondered how they had ever lived on such a tight budget in the past.

Chapter Four

Saturday night, Lizzy and Matt went out on a date to the local *Englisher* restaurant in town. Whenever they went out to eat, it was a treat, but today seemed somewhat less of a thrill. With all the money that Lizzy had been spending on fancy food to cook at home, the meal seemed rather boring.

Once they had finished eating, the waitress came by and asked, "Do you want to order some desert?"

Looking at Lizzy with a smile, Matt announced, "I guess we'll take a piece of chocolate cake with ice-cream. We're splitting it, so we'll need an extra plate."

"*Ach*, Matt, sharing is such a bother." Lizzy couldn't hide her disgust at the thought of being frugal, "Let's get one for each of us!"

"Lizzy," Matt reached out and put his hand over hers, his tone little more than a whisper, "I don't have the money..."

"Don't worry about paying for it, Matt," Lizzy announced, digging through her black purse for some money, "I'll be covering the bill tonight."

Looking up at the waitress, Matt said, "Just give us one. If we need more, I'll buy a second."

The waitress looked uncomfortably from Matt to Lizzy and then back to Matt. Taking a deep breath, she nodded her head, "I'll put in the order for one. Just flag me down if you decide to get two."

As soon as she had left them alone, Lizzy found herself rolling her eyes, "Come on, Matt! What's the matter? I said I have the money. Why can't you let me pay for it myself?"

Matt shook his head slowly, "Lizzy, you don't understand. I don't want to have a girlfriend that pays for her own food. I like saving back my money and bringing you out to eat."

Unwilling to cause a scene or risk totally running their time together, Lizzy gave a curt nod and ended the conversation.

When the waitress delivered their cake, they ate in silence. Lizzy simply could not understand why her boyfriend was so stubborn!

"I'm sorry we fought in the restaurant," Matt whispered when they had finished eat and were seated side-by-side on his buggy, "I don't want us to ever argue about anything. Will ya forgive me...and still let me bring you to the young peoples' meeting Sunday night?"

Lizzy couldn't help but smile. Staying mad at her boyfriend wasn't worth the effort. Sliding over closer to him, she took a deep breath, "I'm sorry, too. *Ach*, Matt, I never would have brought up paying for it if I knew it was going to make you upset." Leaning her head against his shoulder, she took a deep breath of the night air and wished that there was some way that he, too, could enjoy the money her family had been given.

The next morning, Lizzy, Grandpa, and Abe went to church at Joe Eicher's house. Like all Amish people, the community met every other week at one of the homes of an Amish family. Preparing for the church service was a huge event that generally involved hours of cleaning and set-up.

On the way to the Eicher's house, Lizzy noticed Grandpa eyeing various things along the road. When they went past the Amish schoolhouse, he slowed the buggy down to a crawl as he pointed out the sagging roof and needed repairs.

During they church service, Lizzy watched Grandpa stare absent-mindedly at his hands. As bishop of their Amish community,

Grandpa was not in charge of preaching but rather helped the entire group stay true to their beliefs.

Once they had sung the last song and church was ready to end, Grandpa stood up and raise a hand in the air.

"Before we go out to eat this delicious meal, I have an announcement to make," Grandpa said.

At his words, women stopped gathering their children and everyone returned to their seats to listen quietly to what their leader had to say.

"As everyone here knows, I've never been a rich man," Grandpa announced, "So you can imagine my surprise this past week when I discovered that I have inherited a large sum of money."

Lizzy listened as the Amish began to whisper and buzz with excitement.

"Driving past the school house today, I noticed that it needs some serious repairs." Reaching into his billfold, Grandpa pulled out a check, "That's why I want to call Teacher Simon forward to receive a check for twenty-thousand dollars to make the necessary repairs."

Everyone gasped and then began to clap their hands.

"*Wunderbargut*!" Someone yelled out in excitement, "The children won't have to worry about it raining in on their heads any longer!" Everyone laughed.

Giving the congregation a chance to settle down, Grandpa finally announced, "I have something else to bring up, too. I know that this is different, but I want everyone here to take some time to consider this suggestion. My whole life, I've watched the women in our community burdened with the heavy load of hosting church service at their homes. I propose that we step out and build a new church building."

Suddenly, the room went silent.

Build a church? Even to Lizzy, the idea sounded strange and terribly English! Although she saw nothing wrong with the big, impressive churches in the towns, it wasn't their way at all. The Amish were simple folks and holding church within the homes was a tradition that went back hundreds of years.

As the minutes ticked by, there was still no reply to his suggestion. Finally, Joe Eicher stepped up, uncomfortably putting his hands in his pockets and refusing to look at Grandpa, "We'll have a chance to talk about all these things later. For now, my wife invites you outside to have a picnic in our front yard."

Chapter Five

Grandpa didn't stay for the picnic; instead he suggested that they stop at the restaurant in town to buy some food. Lizzy missed the feeling of togetherness she got when she gathered with her friends and family, but certainly wasn't sad to avoid the awkward stares of the others in her community.

That night, Matt pulled his buggy into their driveway at five o'clock. Lizzy had purchased some pre-made hamburger patties in town and had just finished frying them up for her Grandpa and Abe. She would eat at the young peoples' gathering.

"You're making me hungry already," Matt playfully moaned as he leaned over her shoulder. Picking up the box the patties came in, he announced, "*Ach*, we never buy these – too expensive for us poor folks." Although his words were said as a joke, Lizzy noticed something akin to scorn in his voice.

"Who could be here?" Lizzy wondered as she noticed three buggies full of Amish men pull into their drive.

Matt gave a shrug, "Looks like some of the preachers and leaders of the community."

Although she knew it was wrong to spy, Lizzy watched the men hitch their horses to the post by the porch and then step through the front door.

"Hello, Abe," she heard the men greet her brother as they walked through the front door, "Where is your grandpa?"

Lizzy picked up the plate of hamburgers and took them to the table where Grandpa was sitting just as Abe led the group of men into the room.

"Hello there, Mose," the men greeted Grandpa, "Sorry to interrupt your meal."

"No worries," Grandpa returned, "Take chairs. What's on your minds?"

As the men sat down, Lizzy and Matt stepped back into the corner, anxious to see what would happen and hoping not to be sent out of the room.

"*Ach*, Mose," one of the men finally said, "Have you plumb lost your mind?"

"Easy now, Enos," another spoke up, "Mose, we were so thankful for your contribution to the schoolhouse, but I'm afraid that I'm with Enos in asking, what were you thinking when you brought up building a church? You know that isn't the Amish way!"

Grandpa raised an eyebrow, "Come on, men! You know there's no good reason for us not to have a church building."

"Having church within the homes sets us apart from the *Englicher* world," Sam Yoder announced, "If you pull out one of the threads of our beliefs, soon we'll completely unravel! What will keep us from soon having telephones and electricity?"

"And what would be so wrong with that?" Grandpa exclaimed suddenly. In the fifteen years that Lizzy had lived with Grandpa, she had never seen him so upset about anything. She felt almost frightened as she looked into his angry face and watched as it grew redder by the minute.

The other men's eyes grew large as they stared at him.

"Ach," Grandpa finally stormed, "You don't have to like my suggestions at all, but I'll say this...building a church would help our community, and I *am* going to do it! As the bishop of our community, I have the power and with the money, I have the ability."

If the men had looked surprised before, they were totally speechless now. Finally, Enos Bontrager solemnly announced, "I'm sorry you feel this way, Mose. It seems the money has gone to your brain. You maybe the bishop of our community, but that does not mean that you are above reproach. Take some time to consider this idea of yours. If you don't submit to the Amish ways, I'm afraid the community will be forced to go over your head and inflict the *bann*."

The *bann*. Those dreadful words went through Lizzy's mind over and over again. Although she was sitting beside Matt on his buggy, she couldn't pull her thoughts away from that horrible scene at the kitchen table.

Ach, if the Amish chose to *bann* Grandpa, he would be completely forced from their community. He would not longer be able to eat with them – he would be entirely shunned until he repented publicly.

"What's going on with your grandpa, Lizzy?" Matt asked after taking a deep breath, obviously nervous to bring up the uncomfortable subject, "He used to be one of the easiest-going men I ever knew...now he's just acting ornery about everything!"

Lizzy instantly felt her skin bristle. Who was Matt to call her Grandpa names?

"What's that supposed to mean?" She spoke up.

"Come on, Lizzy!" Matt exclaimed, "He's changed...and you have too! Just within a week, it's like you're both different people. I don't like who you're turning into. If things don't change, he's going to end up leaving the Amish entirely."

Lizzy was so furious, it felt like she was on fire.

"Grandpa is one of the best men I know!" She snapped, "If he wants to build a church building, then I'm completely behind him. If you have a problem with it, then maybe we should stop seeing each other. And, if the Amish are going to be so stubborn that they won't accept his gift, then maybe I don't want to be Amish anymore!"

"Lizzy..."

"Just drive," She snapped, folding her arms across her chest and scooting as far away from her boyfriend as she could.

That night, Lizzy sat in her bedroom, thinking about life as she prepared for bed. Lizzy brushed her hair out slowly and stopped to study herself in the mirror. While mirrors weren't usually found in Amish houses, Lizzy had made a secret purchase over the weekend.

Gazing at herself, she tried to gauge how pretty she was compared to the other Amish girls. But wouldn't she be prettier if she had some of that fine paint the *Englishers* wore on their faces!

Instantly, she pushed the thought away, wishing that she hadn't let it run through her mind.

With all that was going on with her grandfather, she truly wondered if they would be left in the Amish church. What Matt had repeated was what all the Amish were thinking. Grandpa was determined to go forward with his plans to build a church...and the Amish community wasn't going to stand for it. There was a good chance that they might get shunned. If that happened, she wondered what Grandpa would do. Would he turn his back on the Amish way entirely? And, if he did, would she go with him?

"Lizzy, Lizzy," she scolded herself, "What are you a thinkin'? Consider Matt!"

But, the more she considered Matt, the more clouded her thinking became. She had been so certain that he was the man she wanted to marry and spend the rest of her life beside, but the money had changed everything.

Lizzy was beginning to like the feeling that money gave her. It made her happy to know that she and her family were a step above the rest of those in their community. She was tired of the work that she had to do as an Amish woman.

If they left the Amish, she would be free to own a washing machine and a drier, a refrigerator, and even a television! Putting aside her brush, Lizzy ran her hand through her hair and took a deep breath.

She was almost scared of what tomorrow might bring.

Chapter Six

All Monday morning, Lizzy found herself looking out the window, afraid that she would see more of the church leaders coming up the drive. In some ways she was frightened, while in others she was almost hopeful.

Grandpa sat at the table, working on a design for the new church. Since the Amish community was set against having it built, he had already contacted a team of English carpenters who could do the work.

That afternoon, someone finally did come up the drive. When Lizzy saw that it was Matt, she couldn't decide if she was more relieved or disgusted.

"Lizzy," Matt took off his straw hat and twisted it between his hands when she invited him inside, "Could we go on a walk and talk?"

Preparing for a lecture, Lizzy braced herself and started across the yard beside him.

Suddenly, Lizzy was surprised when she looked up at Matt and noticed tear drops running down his cheeks. Instantly, her defenses were down and her heart filled with worry for this man she loved so much.

"What's wrong Matt?" Lizzy asked as she reached out to pat her boyfriend on the arm,

"Lizzy," Matt took a deep breath and let it out, "I don't know what to say. My *maam's* finally going to come home, but now the hospital wants us to start paying our bills. She's got to keep taking treatments and they're expensive, too. Dad doesn't even know how he's going to do it at all. He's talking about selling the farm."

"Selling the farm!" Lizzy exclaimed, "What would you all do then?"

"*Daed's* talking about moving back to Pennsylvania. There's nothing for us here if we have to sell everything. We can move in with my grandparents until mom's treatments are finished."

"Surely there will be some other way…"

"Lizzy, my dad already took out a gigantic mortgage on the farm. He's not going to be able to pay it back." Shrugging, Matt announced, "I don't know when we're likely to move, but I'd like the little bit of time we have left together to be good. I'm sorry about last night."

"No, I'm sorry," Lizzy whispered. Reaching out, she wrapped her arms around her boyfriend and pulled him close to her.

That night, Lizzy picked up some food at the restaurant because she didn't feel like cooking. Her heart felt so heavy whenever she thought about Matt and his family. She told Grandpa and Abe. Suddenly, they were no longer concerned about building fancy churches or fighting with the Amish. They just sat together silently, each lost in sorrow over the situation of Matt's family.

"I wish that there was something we could do," Abe muttered softly, "I've always though a lot of Matt's family."

"*Ach*," Grandpa exclaimed as he slammed his hand against the tabletop, "What on earth are we doing? I always looked down on people who had money and were selfish with it…and yet I find that I'm exactly the same way."

"Grandpa!" Abe looked at him in surprise, "How can you say that you're selfish? All you want to do with your money is good! You want to make a better life for us…and you want to help out the church and the community with buildings. How can that be wrong?"

Grandpa shook his head slowly, "In the midst of all our figuring, did we ever stop to even think to ask the Lord what He would want us to do with this money? No. Instead, we chose to plow ahead and do what we thought was best."

Everyone was silent as they looked down at their plates in deep thought.

"Tonight, this ends!" Grandpa announced, reaching out to take Abe's hand in one of his own and Lizzy's in the other, "Tonight we're turning to the Lord to find out what he wants."

The next morning, Grandpa took the money that Lizzy had left over and went to town.

"Well," Abe muttered softly as he worked alongside his sister in the garden, "I sure did enjoy being rich."

"As did I," Lizzy said with a sigh, "But I think I'll be glad to be plain Lizzy once again."

When Grandpa got home, he came out to the garden to work alongside them.

No one said a word until Abe finally ventured to ask, "Do we have anything left at all?"

Grandpa shook his head, "I paid off all of Matt's family's debts and then gave the rest as a donation to the hospital. I've already been to talk to some of the church leaders and apologized for the entire church building idea."

"How are we ever going to make it now?" Abe grumbled, kicking at a clod of dirt with the toe of his work boots.

Grandpa smiled, "I suppose the way we always have...a lot of pinching pennies and patching up clothes. In the end, we did what that Lord wanted and we did what was best for other people who needed the money much worse than us."

"I never did get my buggy," Abe said with a sigh.

"Ahh...that is true." Grandpa gave the teenager a pat on the shoulder, "How about you and I work on that old buggy together. I think if we put some time into it, we can have it good as new."

"And, when you go courting, maybe you can just tell her to hang on tight before you hit a bump in the road!" Lizzy suggested.

They all laughed, finally able to enjoy one another's company without the distraction of money.

Working together silently, they listened to the sound of the birds chirping overhead and enjoyed the cool breeze drifting through the trees.

Prologue

Lizzy smiled to herself as she sat on the homemade wooden swing on the front porch. Although it had been hard to give up the money, she had to admit that a simple life truly was the right one for her.

Looking up from a page in the book she was reading, Lizzy realized that Matt had pulled his buggy into their yard and was coming toward her.

"Hello, Matt," she announced, wishing that she and her beau had never gone through such a rough spot.

Without saying a word, Matt took a seat on the swing beside her.

"It was your grandpa, wasn't it?" Matt asked slowly as he reached out and took Lizzy's hand in his own, "He was the one who helped to cover my *maam*'s doctor bills, right?"

"Matt..." Lizzy looked down at her feet, trying to decide how much she should even start to share, "Ach, Matt, he doesn't want a bunch of people to know. He wanted to keep it a secret. The way Grandpa looks at it, the money wasn't ours to start with...it was just something that God had loaned us so that we could use it to help others. He got off track because of it...we all did, I'm afraid. I'm sorry that I was so harsh to ya, Matt. It was wrong of me. I let the love of money cloud my thinking. Grandpa reminded us that we should pray about what to do with it, and from that point on, it all just became clear."

Matt shook his head, "That's the kind of man I wish that I could be. Lizzy," he took a deep breath, "I'm no where near as great a man as your grandpa, but I'm going to try my best to be a *gut* Amish man who loves his family, helps his neighbors, and serves the Lord. Would you be willing to go through this journey with me...as my wife?"

Lizzy felt her breath catch in her throat and she wondered if she could even start to speak. After all that had happened between them, she was afraid that Matt would be ready to end their relationship completely. She opened her mouth and words wouldn't come out. Instead, all that would come were tears of joy.

"Oh no," Matt teased jokingly, "Looks like you're not very happy with my question!"

Lizzy threw her arms around his neck and let her warm embrace give her answer. Pulling away from the man that she loved, Lizzy exclaimed, "Ah, Matt, being married to you is going to be better than all the money in the world!"

FINDING EMMA

STEPHANIE SWIFT

Rebecca Miller rubbed her eyes and yawned as the early morning sun peeked through her bedroom curtains. While her husband, Matthew, slept peacefully beside her, she eased up from the bed and tip-toed quietly from the room, closing the door behind her. After changing clothes in the bathroom across the hall, she made her way down the narrow hallway, stopping for just a few seconds to press an ear against her daughter Emma's bedroom door, to make sure she was still sleeping.

She smiled. All was quiet.

Rebecca continued down the hall and entered the last door to the right, which opened into a small kitchen. With any luck, she would be able to get breakfast on the table without any interruptions. She gathered what she needed to make biscuits and set her supplies on the kitchen counter. The stillness in the house was a bit disconcerting and something she wasn't quite used to. For the first three years of their marriage, she and Matthew had been on their own, but now their days were filled with the sound of Emma's laughter and the pitter-patter of tiny footsteps on the hardwood floors.

It had been almost a year since they discovered Emma at the small church in their secluded Amish community outside of Lancaster, Pennsylvania. Someone had wrapped her in a blanket and placed her inside a makeshift basket before leaving her on the front porch of the church. It made Rebecca shudder to think of what could have happened to Emma if she hadn't been found in time.

She and Matthew were the first people to arrive for the Saturday morning service, and after he jumped in their wagon and raced to Lancaster in search of the sheriff, Rebecca took Emma inside the church to keep her warm. There was no note attached to the basket or anything that would give them any inclination as to who Emma belonged to.

When Rebecca lifted her in her arms, Emma opened her eyes and stretched her little arms high over her head. There was an instant bond unlike anything Emma had felt before, but she did her best to brush it aside. After all, the sheriff would find the mother soon and Emma would be on her way. She wondered briefly what might happen if the mother disappeared during the night, never to be found again, and a cold chill raced up her spine. If no other family came forward then Emma might spend the rest of her days inside a foster home, and the thought made her heart ache.

It wasn't long before her friends and neighbors began arriving for the service and soon thereafter Matthew returned with Sheriff Owens. Instead of having their regular Saturday morning prayer service, they were each questioned, and no one knew where baby Emma could have come from. It was one big puzzle with several missing pieces, but the sheriff vowed to get to the bottom of it.

Many of her neighbors volunteered to keep Emma while he tended to his investigation, which immediately put Rebecca on the defensive. All of them had children of their own, but she and Matthew were alone. It seemed only right for the two of them to watch over Emma, especially since they were the first couple to find her, and thankfully, the sheriff agreed. At that time, she was simply referred to as "the baby", but calling her Emma felt as natural as breathing, and so the name stuck.

Rebecca stopped kneading the dough and glanced out the kitchen window. It seemed like a lifetime ago, instead of just one year since the day God brought Emma into their lives. After three weeks with no clues, the sheriff told them he would have to place her in foster care, but she and Matthew wouldn't hear of it. The process was long and arduous, but they were allowed to adopt Emma, so it was certainly worth it.

"*Gute mariye.*"

Matthew's deep voice startled her from her daydream, and she smiled at him as he slowly ambled his way to the kitchen table. He was dressed in his work clothes and his hair was neatly combed, but there was no hiding the dark circles under his eyes and the way his shoulders slumped after he sat down. He resembled a man with the weight of the world on his back, and after Emma placed the biscuits in the oven, she wiped her hands on her apron and joined him at the table.

"*Liebchen*, I wish you would get some rest."

He reached for her hands and when he closed his around hers, the calluses on his skin were like a dagger to her heart. His hands were rough, and there were several deep cuts on his palms. Rebecca gently caressed the wounds while holding back tears. She was thankful God had intervened and brought Emma into their lives, but the extra work Matthew took on to put food on their table was more than any one person should bear.

"I don't need rest, *liebchen*. I need to make sure my family is provided for. That's what matters most," he replied.

Rebecca smiled at the endearment. So stubborn but such a heart of gold. When he raised her hands to his lips, she felt a warm rush trickle through her veins that made her tremble. They sat there for the longest while, just enjoying each other's company, until the oven timer rang and interrupted the silence.

"I'll get Emma," Matthew said.

When he left the room, Rebecca removed the biscuits from the oven and placed them to the side so she could scramble some eggs. Moments later she heard heavy footsteps enter the kitchen again, but Matthew wasn't carrying Emma. His eyes were wide and the color had drained from his complexion.

"What's wrong? Where's Emma?" she asked.

He shook his head, but he didn't say anything right away, which alarmed her even more.

"She's not in her room."

Rebecca's breath caught and held for several painful seconds. At that moment, everything stopped, and the fear that consumed her body made her heart race out of control.

"What do you mean? I went in her room and checked on her during the night, and she was sound asleep in her crib."

He didn't answer her, and as she walked past him and made her way to Emma's bedroom, he exited the house through a side door in the kitchen. It wasn't long before she could hear him frantically calling Emma's name.

Her room was empty and deathly quiet. Her blanket was folded neatly and placed in a corner of the crib, and her favorite doll lay on top of it. The mattress appeared as if it hadn't been slept on. Rebecca ran from the room and searched the rest of the house, but Emma was nowhere to be found.

Matthew returned, his breathing labored and tears welling in the corners of his eyes. They met each other in the kitchen and when he grabbed her forearms, she could feel his hands shaking. "I checked the barn and the field, and she's not outside. Go next door and ask Joseph and Amy to help you search while I ride to Lancaster and find Sheriff Owens. I'll be back as soon as I can."

As he raced to the barn to retrieve one of their horses, Rebecca slipped on a jacket and made the long trek across the field to her neighbor's house. She tried not to dwell on how the temperature had dropped now that they were closing in on November. She didn't want to consider the possibility that Emma might be outside in the harsh elements – that she might be crying and calling out for her at that very moment. The thought made her feel sick inside.

Thankfully, Amy and Joseph were home, and when she filled them in on what was happening, they sent one of their older children to round up more people to join in the search. Within a matter of minutes, several of her friends and neighbors converged on her property to try and help locate Emma. Although they did their best to keep her hopes up by offering words of encouragement, Rebecca couldn't shake the uneasy feeling that settled in her heart and refused to let go.

* * * *

The soft strains of Lovina Morgan's lullaby filled the tiny space surrounding her as she rocked her daughter in her arms. She glanced once more around the living room, and pride swelled in her chest over what she'd accomplished in just a few short days. After her grandmother's passing five months prior, she'd worked hard to get everything ready for her baby's homecoming.

"What shall I name you?" she whispered.

Lovina brushed her fingertips against her chubby cheek, enjoying the softness of her skin. The dimples in her cheeks reminded her of the baby's father, and for a split second her smile faded. She felt her joy begin to wane, so she quickly thought of something else to clear the troubled thoughts from her mind. Her ex-boyfriend wasn't worth thinking about, especially after the way he'd thrown her to the wayside once he found out she was pregnant.

Her grandmother's demeanor was much the same way. She couldn't believe her only granddaughter, the one she'd raised since her parents abandoned her at two years old, could do such a vile thing. After all, she was only sixteen years old. What would their neighbors think? Worse yet, what would their Pastor and the rest of the congregation at their church do if they found out? They would become the talk of the town and she *would not* let that happen.

Thus, began a very long pregnancy, locked behind closed doors and away from the rest of the world. Her grandmother wouldn't even consider helping her raise the baby. The thought that she would even want to keep the child was ludicrous. Not long after the baby was born, her grandmother was the one who whisked her away during the night and left her with strangers.

"We'll never be apart again. I promise," she soothed.

Now that her grandmother was gone, she didn't have to worry over them being separated ever again, and she could finally start living her life. The only thing left to worry about were her neighbors. How would she ever live a peaceful life with her daughter without raising suspicion?

* * * *

Sheriff Owens scribbled something inside a notepad he pulled from his shirt pocket, but Rebecca could care less what he wrote. They'd rehashed the details over and over again until she was numb inside. The sun was setting in the west, and most of her neighbors had returned home with heavy hearts and teardrops staining their cheeks. The K-9 unit from Lancaster was brought in to comb the woods behind their home, but hours passed and Emma was still missing.

When one of the K-9-unit officers returned Emma's blanket, after the dogs weren't able to pick up her scent, she buried her face in the soft fabric and wept. She could still smell the lavender soap she used to bathe Emma and a whisper of baby powder, and the fragrance squeezed her heart and nearly consumed her with grief.

"Mr. and Mrs. Miller, are you sure there isn't anyone you can think of who might be angry with you? Someone who would do this to try and get back at you for some reason?"

They both shook their heads. What a ridiculous question. Who could they have angered? They were dear friends with everyone in their community, and they rarely mingled with the English people in Lancaster, except for Sheriff Owens and a couple of the shop owners who bought their homemade goods to sell in their stores.

"What about Emma's birth mother or father? Has anyone tried to contact you?" he inquired.

She and Matthew looked at each other, and she could see the panic in his eyes, which mirrored her own. She'd never considered the possibility Emma's disappearance might have something to do with her biological parents. They'd had Emma so long, and she'd become such a huge part of their lives, she rarely thought about the circumstances that brought them together. Perhaps her birth mother or father – or both – decided to come back and look for her. The thought paralyzed Rebecca with fear.

"We haven't talked to anyone outside our community about Emma except you and your officers," she replied.

Her voice sounded tired – and foreign – even to her own ears. Rebecca crossed her arms over her chest and rocked back and forth on her heels. She needed to be doing something and not standing there like a knot on a log, constantly going over details with Sheriff Owens and his men. Her daughter counted on them to keep her safe, and she knew in her heart they were letting her down.

"We found a fresh set of footprints beneath Emma's bedroom window. They're small, so it's possible we're dealing with a female perpetrator. Did you leave your windows and doors unlocked last night?"

She and Matthew looked at each other again as her eyes filled with tears.

"*Yah*, it's possible," Matthew answered. "Sheriff Owens, we all know each other here. We worship together, we help one another, and we trust each other. If our doors and windows were unlocked it's because we feel safe here amongst our own."

The sheriff closed his notepad and put it and his pen back inside his shirt pocket. "Until now?"

His question made her heart thump erratically inside her chest. *Neh*, he would never make herself believe that one of their neighbors would do this to them. It was incomprehensible.

"We're going to do everything we can to find Emma and return her safely to you. I promise. I have my men canvasing every store in Lancaster, and I'll be sending one of my officers to keep watch here tonight, just in case the suspect decides to return. Don't hesitate to let me know if you think of anything that might help us find out who did this."

She and Matthew nodded in agreement as Sheriff Owens and his men returned to their vehicles and headed back to town. As soon as they were out of view, Matthew pulled Rebecca into his embrace. The floodgates opened and her tears began to fall as the worry and stress from the day's events rippled through her body and left her weak.

"What if something terrible has happened to her, Matthew? What if she's..."

He pressed a finger to her lips and stopped her from continuing. "Don't say it. Don't even think it. We've got to hold fast to our faith and pray that God will return her to us."

She didn't reply. Instead, she collapsed against his chest and let the tears continue until she couldn't possibly cry anymore. She could tell he was being strong and holding himself together for her sake, but she knew he was suffering inside just as much as she was. She couldn't remember a time when she'd ever felt so helpless.

"Rebecca?"

She turned in the direction of the soft, feminine voice and found her good friend, Karen, walking over to join them.

"Come inside," Karen urged. "It's getting cold, and some of the women and I made you two some dinner. I know you probably don't feel like eating right now, but you need to keep your strength up."

When Karen wrapped an arm around Rebecca's waist, she didn't try to resist. As the three of them walked back to the house, she sent up a silent prayer to God, begging and pleading for Him to return their daughter home...safe.

* * * *

Lovina woke the next morning on the living room sofa, unable to recall how she'd gotten there in the first place. Her eyes darted around the room in search of her baby, and she breathed a sigh of relief when she found her laying in her crib on the other side of the room. She could very faintly hear her cooing.

Lovina sat up slowly and massaged her pounding temple. It wasn't the first time she'd lost track of time and over the past month or so it happened quite frequently. Lovina stood and walked across the room. When she leaned over the side of the crib and caught her little one playing with her bare toes, she couldn't help but smile. She was so beautiful. Every little feature from her wavy brown hair to her chubby little feet was perfect.

Unfortunately, she still hadn't been able to come up with a suitable name. She thought about naming her after her grandmother, but thought better of it since the elderly woman was the main reason they were separated in the first place. Lovina gently wrapped her fingers around one of her baby's hands, which made her giggle in response, and the sound was a soothing balm to her soul.

She was almost out of milk, so she would have to go to the grocery store soon, but Lovina knew she couldn't risk taking the baby with her – at least, not right now. She would just have to wait until her nap time, and then she would sneak away and make the half mile trek to the grocery store and back while she slept.

Lovina picked up the baby and rested her against her hip. As she walked into the adjoining kitchen and pulled a jar of baby food from one of the overhead cabinets, she hummed softly and smiled. Her life and purpose was starting to make sense again...at last.

* * * *

Rebecca put on her shoes and placed a white bonnet on top of her head, tying the ribbons securely under her chin so the wind wouldn't unravel them on her drive to Lancaster.

"Where are you going?"

She turned to face Matthew, who had just come inside after spending the past thirty minutes or so talking to the officer who had spent the night in his car in their driveway. Now that he was finally on his way back to the precinct, she could leave without worrying over being followed.

"I'm going to Lancaster to see if they've come across any clues. I can't just sit here and do nothing, Matthew. It's driving me mad."

He grabbed his jacket from the coat rack beside the front door and put it on. Neither of them had slept a wink the night before, and sitting in Emma's room, clutching her doll and blanket to her chest only multiplied the agony that held her close and wouldn't let go. She had to do something before she completely fell apart.

"I'm going with you," he replied.

Rebecca didn't argue with him as he followed her outside to their horse and wagon. When he climbed onto the seat and took the reins, she settled in beside him, and neither of them spoke on the ride to town. She knew he was consumed by his own thoughts and worries, just as she was, so she didn't intervene and try to force him into a conversation. Honestly, she didn't feel like talking. They'd spent the past 24 hours doing nothing but talking – to their neighbors, to Sheriff

Owens, and everyone else who'd worked so hard to help them. Now was the time for action.

As they entered the city limits of Lancaster, Rebecca scoured every face on the crowded streets and sidewalks and peered inside every vehicle they passed. When Matthew steered the horse and wagon into a parking space in front of the precinct, she wasted no time and quickly descended the steps.

"I'll check the supermarket and clothing stores while you talk to Sheriff Owens," she said.

Before she could walk away, Matthew grabbed her hand. "Wait and I'll go with you."

The concerned look on his face melted her heart, and when she lovingly tucked a stray tendril of his hair under his hat, he closed his eyes and pressed her hand to his cheek.

"There's no need for us both to talk to Sheriff Owens. I'll be fine. After you talk to him, come find me and we'll both keep looking."

He gave her a solemn nod before letting her go and making his way inside the precinct. Since there were two clothing stores nearest to the station, she decided to look there first. With it being Saturday, Lancaster was especially crowded, and as Rebecca veered her way through the throng of people, she kept her eyes peeled for anyone or anything that looked suspicious.

She saw several women with babies, and the sight made her heart hurt. She peered inside every stroller and baby carrier she came upon, trying not to appear too obvious or raise a red flag. Her pulse raced each time she saw a brunette baby from behind, but her hopes were dashed time and again when they turned around and she discovered it wasn't Emma.

The clothing stores were filled to overflowing, but the supermarket wasn't nearly as bad. Rebecca took a cart from the line at the front of the store so she could blend in with the crowd, and as she wheeled it around the store, her positive outlook began to diminish. Most of the people in the supermarket were older couples and the younger ones weren't accompanied by children.

When she turned the corner of the baby products aisle for the fifth time, she came upon a young woman standing in front of the jarred baby food, carefully picking up each one and turning them around in her hands so she could read the labels. She couldn't have been more than eighteen or nineteen years old, and she was barefoot.

Seeing people walk around town without shoes wasn't an uncommon occurrence, but something about the woman stopped her in her tracks. Her clothes were disheveled and since her feet were covered in dirt, she guessed she didn't live within the city limits, which were filled with paved roads as far as the eye could see.

Rebecca remained at the opposite end of the long aisle and rummaged through some items on the shelves so the woman wouldn't catch her staring. Every so often Rebecca would steal a glance in her direction, but the woman seemed more focused on reading labels than anything else around her. When she put some jars inside her cart and walked away, Rebecca quickly followed suit, staying just far enough behind her so she wouldn't be spotted.

The woman stopped at the dairy case and grabbed a gallon of milk before making her way to the front of the store where the cashier was located. Emma replaced her cart and left the store, walking hurriedly in the direction of the precinct. When she was within a few feet of it, the door opened and Matthew and Sheriff Owens walked outside. Rebecca's breath was ragged as she approached them, and when she motioned for them to follow her, they didn't ask questions.

The three of them stepped between their wagon and a parked vehicle where they couldn't be seen, and Rebecca quickly filled them in on the young woman she noticed in the supermarket. They watched and waited, and when she saw her leaving the store, she grabbed Matthew's arm.

"That's her!" she exclaimed.

Sheriff Owens nodded, and as they watched the woman walk away in the opposite direction, he turned to face them. "I've seen her before. She lives outside of town in a mobile home park on Curry Lane. She used to live with her grandmother, but she died a few months ago."

Rebecca felt her heart pounding in her ears. "Does she have any children?"

Sheriff Owens thought for a moment before shaking his head. "Not that I'm aware of. Why?"

Matthew looked back and forth between the two of them, but he didn't interrupt. Rebecca felt a small twinge of hope, but she did her best to keep it to a small ember, not wanting to get her hopes up too high in case they were extinguished again.

"She had several jars of baby food and a gallon of milk in her cart."

The sheriff put a hand on his hip and splayed the other one through his thick mane of black hair. "She could be buying them for someone else."

Rebecca fervently shook her head. "Please, Sheriff Owens. I have a very bad feeling about this woman."

He leaned forward and kept his voice low so the townspeople walking past them couldn't overhear. "Mrs. Miller, I can't just search her home without probable cause or a warrant. It doesn't work that way."

Little by little, Rebecca felt her hope dwindling, but she wouldn't be swayed. "There's got to be something we can do. Can't you assign someone to follow her or watch her home?"

Her voice seemed high and shrill, and she knew she probably sounded panicked, but she couldn't help herself. She *was* frightened. This was her daughter they were talking about, and she would do whatever was necessary to find her. Her hunch might lead them nowhere, but she couldn't just sit by and do nothing. Even if it did turn out to be nothing, she would at least know she tried.

"Rebecca, I'm sure they're doing everything they can," Matthew said. His voice was soft and low, and she guessed he was only trying to keep her calm, but it wasn't working.

Sheriff Owens held up a hand. "Hold on. Stay here. I'll be right back."

Without another word, he turned and walked back to the station. A few minutes later he reappeared with a set of car keys dangling from his hand. "Come with me. One of my men will keep an eye on your horse and wagon until we get back."

As he walked to his squad car, Matthew and Rebecca remained right on his heels. After they got inside and buckled themselves in, the sheriff roared the car to life and backed away from the sidewalk. When he turned the wheel in the opposite direction of the young woman, she felt her eyes swell with tears.

"Why are we going this way?" she asked.

The sheriff didn't look at her, but he seemed intent and focused on wherever they were headed. "It will take her awhile to get home, so I'm going to approach from another angle. If we pass her on the dirt road she lives on, she might get suspicious and bolt."

It made sense, but now Rebecca was overwhelmed by the realization that if the young woman *was* the kidnapper, Emma was probably alone inside her home. Watching her buy the baby food and milk gave her hope that Emma was still alive, but that didn't quell the fear that something terrible might happen to her while the woman was away. It scared her even more to think that she may have left her with an accomplice who might hurt her...or worse.

Sheriff Owens took them down several country backroads until he finally came to a stop behind a tall row of hedge bushes on Curry Lane. Ahead of them was a cluster of mobile homes in a large type of subdivision. There were several children playing outside, but she didn't see Emma. When Matthew slid his hand across the back seat and grasped hers, she squeezed him tight and gave him a weary smile.

"There she is."

She and Matthew followed Sheriff Owen's gaze, and her heart began to race as she watched the woman walk through the group of dilapidated mobile homes before climbing the steps of a front porch on a trailer closest to the back of the lot. She unlocked the front door and went inside and several minutes passed without another glimpse of her.

Sheriff Owens removed a cell phone from a pocket in his trousers and started pressing some numbers while Rebecca and Matthew looked on expectantly. "Robert?" he said. "You can approach the premises now."

* * * *

Lovina wiped the baby's mouth and attempted one last time to feed her the pureed banana baby food, but she wouldn't hear of it. Every time she came near her mouth with the spoon, she would turn her head at the last minute and pound her little fists on top of the highchair before Lovina eventually gave up.

"Okay, so I need to mark bananas off the list too."

She'd managed to feed her peaches and peas, but bananas and prunes were definite deal breaker's. Lovina grabbed a dish towel from one of the kitchen drawers and tried to clean up the mess on the highchair and the baby's hands, but it wasn't an easy task. Lovina learned quickly how much she loved playing with her food, since most of it ended up on the highchair and in her hair and lap instead of in her mouth.

"I really need to give you a name. What do you think of Claire?"

She was surprised when the baby looked up at her and grinned as if she understood.

"Then Claire it is."

A loud knock on the front door startled them both, and Lovina gave the baby her pacifier, hoping it would keep her quiet. Lovina tip-toed to the front window near the door and pulled the curtain aside. A tall gentleman stood on her front porch. He carried a manila envelope in his hands, and she could just barely make out an employee nametag clasped to his shirt and Anderson Electric & Gas stitched on the front pocket.

Lovina expelled a sigh of relief. She recognized the name from the many times her grandmother made service calls to the company, but she couldn't remember calling them since her death. Then again, there were a lot of things she was unable to recall lately, due to her blackouts, which were steadily getting worse.

Lovina looked around the park, but nothing appeared out of the ordinary. She glanced one last time at the baby before making her way to the front door, and when she opened it, the man waved and smiled.

"Hello. Are you Miss Lovina Morgan? I'm Robert Thornton from Anderson Electric & Gas. We've received some calls from this neighborhood about a possible gas leak, and I was sent to check the homes in this area for damage." He opened the manila folder and pulled out a piece of paper. "Do you still have the gas stove and furnace?"

Lovina nodded, but she couldn't recall smelling a gas leak or hearing her neighbors complain about one.

"Would you mind if I check them? I promise it will only take a couple of minutes, and I will be out of your hair in no time."

He smiled again and his friendly demeanor put her at ease. When she opened the door, and motioned for him to come inside, he thanked her before pointing to the kitchen. "I'll check the stove first."

As he walked toward the kitchen, Lovina stayed close behind him. When he noticed the baby, he spoke briefly to her before making his way to the stove. He pulled it away from the wall to check the valve behind it, and she remained by the door and watched. It didn't take long for him to examine both the stove and the furnace, and within ten minutes or so, he was walking toward the front door.

"Thank you so much, Miss Morgan. I didn't notice any problems, but we'll keep monitoring the area until we can find out where the source of the leak is coming from. I hope you have a pleasant afternoon."

Lovina opened the front door, and as he walked to his vehicle, he turned to wave one last time before getting in and slowly making his way down the drive and away from her neighborhood.

* * * *

Rebecca held her breath as a black vehicle pulled up alongside them and stopped. Sheriff Owens got out and talked briefly to the man behind the wheel before opening the back door of the squad car and asking her and Matthew to step outside.

"This is Robert Thornton, a good friend of mine. Your hunch was right. There's a baby matching Emma's description inside, and she's safe for the time being, but we need to get her out quickly. Robert will be taking you back to the precinct."

Relief flooded through Rebecca as she furiously shook her head. "I want to go with you. She needs me."

Before Sheriff Owens could object to her request, Matthew put his arms around her waist and started leading her toward Robert's car. "We're wasting time, Rebecca. We need to let the man do his job."

She knew he was right, but the realization that the woman may do something to harm her daughter once she realized what was going on terrified her to her very core.

"I'll do my best to return her safely to you," Sheriff Owens replied. "Just please do as I ask."

Matthew opened the passenger door and helped her inside before sliding in next to her. While Rebecca watched from the rear window as the sheriff got back in his squad car, Robert sped away from the scene and carried them both to safety.

* * * *

Lovina Morgan looked...lost.

Emma was returned to Rebecca and Matthew unharmed, and although she probably should have felt anything but compassionate, Rebecca knew in her heart that God would want her to forgive Lovina. The young woman sat perfectly still on a bench inside the jail cell with her legs dangling over the side. When she looked up and noticed Rebecca standing nearby, she never flinched.

"I wasn't going to hurt her," she remarked, softly.

Rebecca moved closer and wrapped her hands around the cold steel bars. "I believe you."

She'd already heard the facts from Sheriff Owens after he'd spent two hours interrogating Lovina. She knew about the numerous bottles of prescription medication the officer removed from her home, and she overheard the sheriff tell Matthew how Lovina had been sick throughout most of her life – mentally and physically.

Rebecca knew these things, but she wanted to talk to her alone...mother to mother...and draw her own conclusions.

"My grandmother was a midwife," Lovina continued. "She delivered several babies in your community, and when she found out I was pregnant, she told me from the very beginning that my baby would be sent there to live."

There was so much sadness in her voice – a profound, heart wrenching sadness that was unmistakable.

"I realize now she was just doing what she felt was best to give the baby...to give Emma...the best life possible. I know you might find this hard to believe, but I'm thankful she's with you and your husband."

When Lovina started crying, Rebecca swallowed hard to keep her own tears at bay.

"I know I'm not well. I can't take care of Emma, but I know she's going to have such a great life. Thank you for taking her in and caring for her when I couldn't. I'm so sorry for what I put you through, and I hope someday you'll be able to forgive me."

Rebecca walked over to the side closest to Lovina and extended an arm through the steel bars. She seemed hesitant at first, but it didn't take long before Lovina grasped her hand.

"I do forgive you," Rebecca replied.

She didn't know what the future held for Lovina, but she did know she would want someone kind to reach out to her if the situation was reversed. Her troubled spirit was broken – there was no denying it.

"I know it's probably too much to ask, but when Emma is older will you please tell her I loved her?"

Rebecca squeezed her hand. "Of course, I will."

And she would do whatever it took to keep her promise. After all, Lovina Morgan was the first woman in Emma's life, and the first soul who loved her...and that would never change.